HOTSHOTS

HOTSHOTS

A NEIL HAMEL MYSTERY

BY THE AUTHOR OF *PARROT BLUES*

JUDITH
VAN GIESON

HarperCollins*Publishers*

HarperCollins books may be purchased for educational, business, or sales promotional use. For information please write: Special Markets Department, HarperCollins Publishers, Inc., 10 East 53rd Street, New York, NY 10022.

FIRST EDITION

Designed by Christine Weathersbee

Library of Congress Cataloging-in-Publication Data
Van Gieson, Judith, 1941–
    Hotshots : a Neil Hamel mystery/Judith Van Gieson.—1st ed.
        p. cm.
    ISBN 0-06-017512-5
    1. Hamel, Neil (Fictitious character)—Fiction. 2. Women lawyers—New Mexico—Albuquerque—Fiction. 3. Albuquerque (N.M.)—Fiction.
    I. Title.
    PS3572.A42224H68 1996
    813'.54—dc20   96-12540

96 97 98 99 00 ❖/RRD 10 9 8 7 6 5 4 3 2 1

This book is dedicated to the memory of the fourteen
firefighters who died fighting the South Canyon fire
on Storm King Mountain, Glenwood Springs, Colorado,
July 6, 1994

And to the memory of Dwight A. Myers,
New Mexico's much-loved and deeply missed bookman

ACKNOWLEDGMENTS

Many thanks to Gaye Brown and Al Gonzales for filling in the blanks in my knowledge; to attorney Alan M. Uris for his legal advice; and to James Peña and John Herron for expressing the power, the terror, and the poetry of fire fighting. A special thanks to David V. Holtby for sharing his knowledge of fire fighting and the pain of his family's terrible loss.

1

It was beginning to feel like the year it rained twice. We never have a lot of rain in Albuquerque, but last spring there was none. When May turned to June it got hot. Rattlesnakes slithered onto West Mesa terraces, bears came out of the mountains searching for food or drink, and coyotes crisscrossed the foothills trolling for pets. Most years when the heat arrives the wind dies down, but this summer it continued, blowing West Mesa dirt across town, turning wandering trash bags into flapping black ravens, swirling dust devils down back roads and driveways, scratching branches against skylights, turning your mind into a house with wide-open windows. My lover, the Kid, is sometimes known as El Greñas, the mophead, but even his hair went flat in the dry heat. My secretary, Anna, kept her hairdo's volume up, but it took hours in the bathroom spraying and teasing.

A controlled burn in the Cibola National Forest got out of control and the smoke drifted one hundred miles east to town. The air turned as gritty as a winter night when everyone's fireplace is cranking out smoke. It tasted like too many Marlboros and smelled like an overbooked campground. Mechanics playing with fireworks in Melloy Dodge's paint-storage room set the place on fire and it erupted in a cumulonimbus of black smoke.

In May the fires start in the southern New Mexico forests, the Lincoln and the Gila. Ignited by dry lightning strikes and exacerbated by squirrelly winds, they follow summer north, flanking the Rockies, spotting into Colorado, Utah, Wyoming, and Montana. It happens every year, a cycle as sure as life, aging, and death. But last summer's fires became history: the Capitan, the Black Range, the Weed, the fire on Thunder Mountain. They burned bigger and hotter than ever, and they didn't go out until snow fell in October.

In mid-June lightning ignited a blaze in the South Canyon of Thunder Mountain twenty miles from Oro, Colorado. It was too early for a Colorado fire, but winter had been mild and by Memorial Day the snowpack had melted into the San Juan River and the Rio Grande, causing class-four rapids and fire conditions that shouted watch out. A fast-moving cold front whipped a small, containable fire into a large, treacherous inferno, and nine Duke City Hotshots (a group of highly skilled wildland firefighters based in Albuquerque) were killed trying to outrun the flames. Four of the nine were young women.

In early August Eric and Nancy Barker, the parents of

Joni Barker, one of the young women who were killed, came to my law office on Lead. By then rain had brought relief and the winds had moved on to Texas. My brain felt like I owned it again. A sense of order had been restored to the Duke City, but the Barkers were refugees from the city of grief. Their eyes were ragged reminders that no matter how tidy your own yard gets there's always another place where death is as sudden and random as lightning.

Nancy strode into the office two steps ahead of her husband. She was an athletic woman about five feet four inches tall who seemed to have an engine running somewhere inside that kept her going. Her hair was blond and short, tamed by hair spray and a razor cut. Her lipstick was bright red and had been carefully applied. She wore jeans, hiking boots, and a T-shirt with a green V-shaped ribbon pinned over her heart. She'd told me she was an elementary school teacher when she'd called to make the appointment.

Her husband, she'd said, taught history at UNM. Eric was several inches taller than Nancy, about five ten. His hair was curly and slivered with gray. He had a thin face with high cheekbones and pale, intelligent eyes. He wore khakis and a rumpled white shirt, and he, too, had a green ribbon pinned over his heart. His aura of grief and despair was almost palpable. Both of them were in their late forties, I figured, barely old enough to have raised a firefighter daughter, far too young to have lost one. They were about ten years older than me, but looked twenty years fitter.

They sat down in the chairs across from my desk and I offered them a choice of drinks—water or coffee. Eric requested coffee with two sugars. Nancy had water. Then I asked why they had come to me; most of the cases that found their way to my law office involved real estate and divorce.

"We heard you were interested in environmental issues," Nancy said.

There were plenty of those in New Mexico, but in the past the environmental cases I'd handled had involved endangered species. One thing endangered species and fire had in common was that they'd both been heavily managed by government and might have done better if left alone.

"We live in the East Mountains," Nancy added. "We wanted a New Mexico lawyer."

But it had been a Colorado fire. A pack of Marlboros was sitting in my desk drawer, but I picked up a pencil and rolled it around in my fingers instead. "The fire was a terrible tragedy," I said.

"It was," Eric said.

"The green ribbons, are they a tribute to your daughter?"

"Yes. Green is the color of the hard hats the Duke City Hotshots wear."

"What is it you want me to do?" I asked.

Eric stared down at his shoes. Nancy leaned forward. "We want you to sue the government for negligence in Joni's death."

"*She* wants to sue," Eric said.

"You don't?"

My office window with its decorative burglar bars was wide open. Eric was looking out through the bars, but not at the alley or at Lead. He was focusing on some point in the distance, the vanishing point perhaps. "We're already getting a settlement of a hundred and twenty-five thousand dollars from the Forest Service," he said. "Suing for more won't bring Joni back. It'll just drag out the suffering. OSHA is investigating. I think we should let them handle it."

"Do you think one government agency is going to find another one guilty of negligence, Neil?" Nancy snapped. Anger, I saw, was fueling her engine.

"Probably not."

"I don't believe anger is the way out of grief," Eric responded.

For some people it might be, I thought. Nancy's eyes had a spark in them. Eric's were gray and flat. "It's not the money," she said. "I want someone to be held accountable for Joni's death."

It's the basic issue in civil suits. Better to make the guilty party pay or to forgive and forget? Or try to forget if you can't forgive? The answer depends on the aggrieved person and on whether a settlement will make any practical or emotional difference to that person. Both were valid points of view, but, when one couple harbored both of them, the result could be big trouble. I'd spent enough time around feuding couples in my real estate and divorce practice to know how difficult they can be, and this couple seemed evenly enough matched that the opposing points of view would stay that way. It appeared unlikely that either of them would dominate the other. Still, it wasn't every day I was asked to sue the government for negligence. Where the government is concerned there's usually more than enough blame to go around—and there's always an unlimited supply of money.

"I can't represent you in the state of Colorado, but I can in a federal court," I said.

"It's a federal case," Nancy replied. "The U.S. Forest Service and the BLM were in charge."

"Can you tell me why you think there is a case?" I asked her.

"Joni had been on a fire in the Gila for fourteen days without a break, and she was exhausted. She came home for one day, then got the call to go to Thunder Mountain. The hotshots were helicoptered into the fire in the morning with no briefing. There was a cold front moving in, but that fact was never communicated to the firefighters. The only weather information they had came from the weather channel. It's all in the interagency report. I brought you a copy." She handed the report to me.

"Thanks," I said.

"The oldest person on Joni's crew was twenty-eight years old," Nancy continued. She stared straight ahead at the white wall behind my desk. Her eyes were dark and focused. "The bodies were burned beyond recognition. The only way to identify them was by dental records."

It would have been enough to make me sue if I'd been a parent.

"It was a very fast-moving cold front," Eric said.

"That canyon was a tinderbox. The firefighters were totally unprepared. They never should have been sent in there," Nancy responded.

"Why were they?" I asked.

"Because nearby homes were threatened," she answered.

"Many of the government's fire-fighting orders were ignored," Eric said. "The crew built a fireline downhill on a steep slope with no designated safety zones or escape routes. That's in the report, too."

"Who was responsible for that?" I asked.

"James Chancellor, the Incident Commander, made some errors," Eric replied.

"What happened to him?"

"He died in the fire."

"If you want to talk about errors. The lookout didn't see the fire blow up in the canyon and warn the hotshots, either." Nancy turned toward Eric. The edge in her voice had gotten noticeably sharper. A cold front was blowing into this marriage.

Eric's eyes had come back into the room, but they'd brought long distance with them. "I don't want to argue about that, Nancy," he said.

"Suit yourself," she responded.

"Hotshots always have the option of saying no if they think an assignment is too dangerous," Eric told me.

"And how often does that happen?" I asked. It seemed to me that a person who would become a hotshot fire-fighter wasn't a person who'd be likely to turn down an assignment because it was dangerous.

"Very rarely," he admitted.

"You know, sometimes you sound like the government, like you're blaming the hotshots for what happened," Nancy said. "The major mistakes were made a lot higher up than on the fireline. That's where the buck ought to stop."

"I'm trying not to blame anybody, Nancy. Sometimes conditions are so severe there's nothing anybody can do. It was a major cold front with winds of forty miles an hour. Nobody could have predicted how fast that fire would blow up. Nobody can control how dry a winter is. Fire fighting is a dangerous and risky business. Every fire-fighter is aware of that when he or she goes on the line." Believing Joni's death had been inevitable seemed to be making this easier for him. Fate was a tent that he was hiding under. "I've been on the line myself. I was a fire-fighter when I was in college," he explained. "Nancy would like to have been, but they weren't hiring women then. Now they're hiring forty percent."

"It's the law," Nancy said. "They're not doing it out of the goodness of their hearts."

"Joni wanted more than anything to be a Duke City Hotshot," Eric said. "She was very good at it and she loved the work. Would she want us to sue the Forest Service?"

"I think she would," Nancy said. "That report blames the victims, and it criticizes the hotshots for their can-do attitude. What kind of attitude would you expect a twenty-two-year-old hotshot to have?"

The same kind of attitude I had when I was twenty-two and felt invincible: what mattered was keeping up with my peers, who felt equally invincible. "Why don't I read this report and see what I think?" I said.

"Okay," they both agreed.

"But you should know that I can't take this case if you're divided. It's going to be a difficult and emotionally draining experience." For them. Although it also had the potential to be very rewarding monetarily for them and me. "The government is going to fight us every step of the way and they've got the resources to do it. It will take a deep commitment from both of you to proceed."

Eric's eyes turned back to the window. "We'll discuss it," Nancy said.

"Is there anyone who was at the fire I could talk to? The hotshots who survived?" I asked.

"Joni's boyfriend, Mike Marshall, was there," Nancy said. "He'll talk to you."

"Anyone else?" I'd hate to base a case on the account of a man who'd seen his girlfriend die.

"Ramona Franklin was a good friend of Joni's," Eric said.

"A great friend. Ramona's the lookout who never saw the fire." Sparks flashed in Nancy's dark eyes.

"Talk to her," Eric said, handing me a strip of paper with an Albuquerque phone number on it. Nancy gave me Mike Marshall's number and a video.

"Some of the people involved were interviewed on TV. I made a video of it," she told me. "The Forest Service offered to fly the families to the site. Mike Marshall is coming, and we've been waiting for the right day. You're welcome to join us when we go."

"Let me read the report first and talk to the other hot-shots. If I think there's a case, I'll come."

They both stood up, thanked me, and turned toward the door. Eric departed two steps ahead of his wife.

2

As soon as they were gone I lit my Marlboro and asked my secretary, Anna, what time it was. I don't wear a watch or hang a clock on the wall, proving, if only to myself, that I'm not a bill-by-the-minute lawyer.

"You're gonna be late," she said.

"How late?"

"Ten minutes if you leave right now."

"That's not late in New Mexico," I said. I had a real estate closing to get to at three-thirty—my own. This time the only half of a squabbling couple I represented was myself. I'd left no time to prepare for the closing, but it didn't matter because there's no way I could ever prepare myself for owning a house. So why was I doing it?

One day when I stopped by to see the Kid at his car repair shop in its new North Valley location I took a different route home and passed a house with a "For Sale" sign on it. It was the right material—adobe. It was the right size—about twice as big as my apartment. And it was the right neighborhood—the part of the North Valley outside the city limits where there are still empty fields, minimal zoning, and a small-town feel.

Usually you have to be either rich or poor to own an adobe house; the materials are cheap, but the amount of labor involved is costly. It's not often one becomes available to the middle class. The house I was buying had been renovated, but not too much. It had Saltillo tile and brick floors, vigas and beams in the ceiling, corbels supporting the beams, and a fireplace shaped like half a beehive. There wasn't a right angle in the place. Even the courtyard had adobe's sinuous walls. In the tradition of adobe houses this one used skylights, walls, and the courtyard to create its own private world. Moving into my adobe reminded me of putting on a veil. It can be a good place to hide out.

The house was one lot away from an irrigation ditch, and the cottonwoods that grew there had branches large enough to support several tree houses. The tiny yard had been landscaped with rosebushes, piñon and juniper, and a drip irrigation system. All I had to do was turn the system on in the spring and off in the fall, my idea of gardening. A white horse grazed in the field behind the house. It could be seen through a place where a tree forked between two fences. There was a double-wide next door and a radio tower down the street. That's what made it affordable; some people prefer a tidier neighborhood, but a street where every house is identical makes me feel trapped.

The house's renovations had been a case of real estate nearly precipitating divorce. The husband had done the work and when he finished his wife had refused to move to the North Valley. He saved his marriage by selling me the house. I smoked three cigarettes on the way to the title company. It was a good house, the price was right. The problem wasn't the property. The problem was ownership—of anything. When you rent an apartment, you can shut the door and walk away. When you own a house, it's always on your mind. Still, the papers got passed. Then I went to my house, sat down on the brick floor, and wondered how I was ever going to fill the space.

Over the weekend the Kid helped me move with his pickup. Nature has a couple of laws about moving, and all of them applied. One: You'll end up arguing with whoever it is that helps you. Two: You always own more than you thought you did. (I could remember when everything I had fit in the back of a hatchback.) Three: You either have far too little or far too much to fill the new space. Four: When it's over, you swear you'll never move again. I had four rooms but barely enough furniture to fill two. The Kid was heading for the second bedroom with an armload of empty boxes when I stopped him.

"They can go in the garage," I said. "That's what garages are for."

"What are you going to put in this room?" he asked.

"Nothing."

"Why?"

"I like it that way." For some people an empty room is a canvas waiting to be filled up, but to me it resembled an open window or a rental car with unlimited mileage and a full tank of gas. I prefer things that remain unfinished.

"Okay." He shrugged.

He took the boxes out to the garage, set up the TV in the other bedroom, poured me a Cuervo Gold, popped open a Tecate, and called it a day.

"To your new house, Chiquita," he said, tipping his beer.

"Thanks," I replied.

He lay down on the bed to watch "Walker, Texas Ranger," his favorite bad TV show. Chuck Norris had killed four bad guys aboard an airplane and was about to take a dive when the Kid fell asleep.

"You awake?" I punched his shoulder, but he groaned and rolled over. The house would have to wait until morning to be broken in. Moving had tired the Kid out, but it left me too wired to sleep.

By now Chuck Norris was diving for the good guy who had been free-falling for several thousand feet. As he swam through the air, grabbed the guy, and popped his chute, I snapped the show off, found Nancy Barker's tape, and inserted it into the VCR.

It was a channel 12 special investigative report on the Thunder Mountain Fire. Kyle Johnson, wearing his trademark suspenders, conducted an in-depth interview with a homeowner who lived near the South Canyon, a middle-aged guy named Ken Roland who had a silver ponytail and a diamond earring in one ear. He was a Californian turned Coloradan, one of those who had fled the formerly golden state. Some Californians end up in New Mexico, more end up in Colorado. Wherever they spread out across the West they increase property values. Compared to California prices, most Western real estate is a Third World bargain.

The camera focused on his trophy home, which was the size of ten houses like mine or one medium-sized hotel. Not a spark had marred the expanse of his cedar-shake roof. The house bordered on a wilderness area and was reachable by a ten-mile dirt road in a Blazer or Mercedes-Benz jeep. It was a private and remote retreat that many people would covet. Kyle Johnson, channel 12's pit bull, was nipping at Roland's heels about the urban/wildland interface and the difficulty of protecting homes in remote areas.

"It's the government's responsibility to protect private landowners from public land fires," Roland said while the diamond earring sparkled in the sunshine. "I'm very grateful to the firefighters for saving my home. It's a terrible tragedy that those young people lost their lives in the fire."

The report continued as Kyle interviewed a hotshot who had escaped the fire. Until the hotshot spoke it was impossible to tell if the face beneath the hard hat belonged to a man or a woman. It was an old face on a young body, a face that had been to the mountain and back, way weary and black with soot. "Nine of my buddies died up there," the hotshot said. "Nobody's house is worth risking a firefighter's life for. Nobody's."

"Chiquita, please," the Kid grumbled, pulling the pillow over his head. I zapped the TV off, lay back, watched the shadow of a branch skate across my skylight, and listened to the sounds a house makes when it thinks no one's listening. Someone tossed ice into a bucket in the freezer. Something scurried above the vigas in the ceiling. A valve in the toilet went whoosh, and I fell asleep.

I know a property manager in Santa Fe who sleeps with her lover in all her new listings. The properties she handles are luxury vacation homes with mind-bending views and absentee owners. They have bathrooms as big as bedrooms and bedrooms as big as a house. She doesn't do it for the movie-star–sized beds, for the skylights with a view of the moon, or even to warm up in the Jacuzzi. She does it for the adventure. She does it because it's forbidden.

I woke up in my own house in my own bed where nothing was forbidden to me, but everything was new. "You awake?" I whispered to the Kid. He wasn't, but I put my arm around his skinny body and woke him up. When we were finished the house had been christened.

I got up to make coffee. Once the bed had been set up last night and the TV plugged in, I'd thought I was moved, but in morning's light I saw how much farther there was to go. It would take a backhoe to clean out the dining area. There were boxes all over the kitchen. How could someone who cooks so little have accumulated so much? I wondered. I found the kettle, boiled some water, and poured it over the instant. I opened the refrigerator, a reflex action. What had I been expecting to find in there but white walls and metal shelves? Nothing that had been in my old refrigerator had been worth moving. Most of it had been unrecognizable. The brat who resided in the ice maker had a tantrum and heaved some ice. "Shut up," I said.

There was a brown box from Pastian's bakery on the top shelf of the fridge. I opened it and found six pineapple empanadas. "Thanks, Kid," I said.

"*De nada,*" he replied. He was dressed in work clothes. As soon as he finished his coffee and empanadas, he headed for the door.

"Where are you going?" I asked him.

"To work."

"On Sunday?"

"*Sí. 'Ta luego.*"

"Bye," I said. Men don't mind helping you move the furniture, but when it comes to unpacking the boxes they're gone. I didn't blame him. I was the one who knew where the stuff ought to go, but I didn't want to put it away either.

I took my coffee, went back to the bedroom, dressed in the jeans and T-shirt I'd worn yesterday (my other clothes were still packed somewhere), and clicked on the VCR.

The next interviewee on the Thunder Mountain Fire report was a Forest Service official who looked bone weary. "It's been a gnarly season, the worst season we've ever had," he said. "We lost nine firefighters here, two in Wyoming, three in California. Three million acres have burned."

"Why has it been such a bad season?" Kyle Johnson asked.

"A number of reasons: a dry winter, a buildup of fuels, a fire-fighting force that's overworked and stretched thin." He stopped himself; he'd been revealing too much, forgetting for a moment that he was on camera.

Kyle didn't give him a chance to gather his wits. "What is the cost to taxpayers?"

"Enormous."

"Is the urban/wildland interface part of the problem?"

"Yes."

"I understand four young women were killed at Thunder Mountain."

"That's true."

"Is it normal for so many members of a crew to be women?"

The official blinked and looked around like he was waking from a bad dream. "When we call for a firefighter we don't care whether we get a man or a woman. What matters is that the individual can do the job. The women firefighters are professionals. They've been challenged and they've proven they can do the work."

The tape ended. I rewound it and went back to the kitchen, where I made myself a cup of Red Zinger with honey. The guy in the freezer was still dropping ice in his bucket and the boxes had not been unpacked. I took my tea to the living room (the room with the least mess), sat down on the sofa, opened the interagency report, and was still reading when the Kid showed up at three. The investigators listed the causes of the fire: a lightning strike, a high fuel buildup, a dry spring, severe winds. They listed the things that had gone wrong: fires were burning all over the West and resources were stretched thin, the change in weather conditions had not been communicated to the hotshots, the lookout had not seen the blowup in time to warn the firefighters, the hotshots had not dropped their packs or deployed their fire shelters when threatened. At the end of the report the investigators interviewed the firefighters, who came up with their own conclusions. The Duke City Hotshots had chosen to be interviewed as a team, so neither Ramona Franklin nor Mike Marshall were quoted directly. That account lost some immediacy in the group telling, but the individual accounts of the other firefighters were vivid and angry. Between the firefighters' statements and the investigators' conclusions lay a gulch wide enough for a lawsuit to fill.

I heard the Kid let himself in through the kitchen doorway. *"Puta madre,"* he swore as he collided with a box. It didn't take him long to track me down in the living room. "You're *reading*, Chiquita?" he asked.

"It's the Forest Service report on the Thunder Mountain Fire. The firefighters came to one conclusion, the investigators came to another."

Without even asking he knew whose side I'd be on. "Are you going to do it?"

"I don't know. The parents are divided. She wants to sue, he doesn't. There are a couple of firefighters I need to talk to before I decide." But he and I both knew that I wanted this case so bad I was already feeling the warmth of the flames and listening for the crackle of the truth. My house was a mess, but my mind was focused.

"That's good, Chiquita, but when are you going to move in?"

"I'll take you to dinner if you help me unload the boxes."

"I don't know where to put things," he protested.

"I'll tell you," I said.

On Monday morning I called Joni's friend, Ramona Franklin, and told her I was Eric and Nancy Barker's lawyer.

"Why do the Barkers need a lawyer?" she asked me. Her voice was soft and she had a way of putting equal emphasis on all the syllables that made me wonder how she got an Anglo surname.

"They want to sue the Forest Service for negligence in Joni's death."

"That won't do any good," Ramona said, weighing carefully every word.

"Nancy Barker feels that if the government was negligent they should be held accountable."

"Why did the Barkers ask you to call me? Why doesn't Mrs. Barker call me herself?"

"She thought you might have observed something at the fire that could help me in preparing a case." As for why Nancy didn't call Ramona herself, I wasn't sure yet. "Would you be willing to meet me and talk about it?"

There was a pause. Long distance was in the line even though I'd dialed a local number. "All right," Ramona said eventually.

"Are you married?" I asked her, wondering if that was where the Anglo name had come from.

"No."

We made arrangements to meet in Java Joe's the following morning. It was a place I knew downtown where you could sit and drink coffee until the pot ran dry or the words ran out.

3

Officially, the Land of Enchantment runs on Rocky Mountain time. Unofficially, New Mexicans operate on their own time. It's the land of the mystic, the artist, the poet, the outlaw, and all of them dance to their own drum. The night I attended my first party in Santa Fe I arrived fashionably (I thought) an hour late. The hostess was still fixing the dip and arranging the flowers. That's Santa Fe time. In Albuquerque we run on orange-barrel time. We have orange-barrel slaloms all over town, and once you enter one you can throw your schedule out the window. One place you'd think would go by the clock is the courtroom, but there's a municipal court judge famous for keeping lawyers and defendants waiting for hours while he waters his roses and feeds the pigeons.

Since I don't wear a watch I've developed my own methods of telling time. I used to be able to lean over and peek at other people's watch faces in restaurants or bars until everybody went digital. Then I learned to go by instinct. I can wake to the minute if I have a plane to catch, but I can't do it on an ordinary day. In my office I had to have Anna tell me when it was ten o'clock, time for my appointment with Ramona at Java Joe's. I took the report along to have something to read in case she was late, but Ramona was already waiting—the only woman alone at a table, the only Indian in the room.

"Ramona?" I asked.

She stood up and extended her hand. "Hello," she said.

"I'm Neil Hamel. Thanks for coming."

Ramona wore glasses with clear rims, a T-shirt without the green ribbon, jeans, and hiking boots. A backpack sat on the floor beside her. She had a strong and sturdy build. Her hair was shoulder length and parted in the middle. Her face was full and solemn. She was finishing up one black coffee; I got her another.

"What did you think of this?" I indicated the report I held.

"I didn't read it."

"Why not?"

"Why?" She shrugged. "It won't change anything."

"It puts a lot of blame on the firefighters."

"That's what people are saying."

"Are you going back on the line?"

"I have to. I'm in school. I have a daughter. I need the money."

"How did you get into fire fighting?" I asked.

"I lost my scholarship. Fires are like cows." Her smile flickered and vanished.

"How's that?"

"You milk them for the money. I work in the summer, get all the overtime I can, and make enough money to go to school in the winter."

"UNM?"

She nodded, staring across the room. I know that some Indians believe it's rude to look people in the eye, but my eyes were drawn to hers anyway. It may well have been rude to ask so many questions, too, but that was my business and so far she'd been answering.

"You were the lookout on the hotshot crew?"

"I was stationed near the ridge top. I didn't see the fire blow up. It crossed the canyon and came out of there howling like a terrible red wolf. The trees were twisting and screaming. It was moving so fast the firefighters didn't even know it was behind them until it was too late. When it hit them, the sawyer was still shouldering his saw." She stared into the dregs of her coffee.

I stood up and got her a refill but didn't get one for myself. I didn't want to get caffeined out. The caffeine didn't seem to have affected Ramona. She'd continued at her own measured pace. "Wasn't there aerial surveillance?" I asked.

"No," she said.

"Should there have been?"

She chose her words carefully. "There usually is."

"Do you think the Forest Service was negligent?"

"I don't know," she said.

"The report said the hotshots would have escaped if they'd dropped their packs."

"It wouldn't have mattered. You can't outrun a fire that's moving faster than a bird can fly." She had her own way of speaking, slow, rhythmic, full of poetic images. "Your courts won't solve anything. The Navajo way is that if you hurt someone, you restore balance by making it up to that person or to the family. The Navajo way is to talk to the elders, but Mrs. Barker won't speak to me."

"She is devastated by Joni's death," I said. It was obvious that to some degree she blamed Ramona for it, but I didn't mention that.

Ramona shifted in her seat when Joni's name was mentioned.

"You're a Navajo?" I asked.

"Yes, but I can't speak Navajo. My parents never spoke it in front of us children. They wanted us to grow up speaking English. We lived in Albuquerque for a while and sold jewelry in Old Town, but after my father died we went back to the Rez near Farmington."

"How old were you then?"

"Ten."

"Your father must have been young if you were only ten."

"He was forty-two."

"My father died when he was forty-eight."

"What killed him?"

"He had a heart attack, but he also drank."

"My father did, too," she said very quietly. "There was a car accident, but there was drinking."

She would have been young enough to experience her

father's death only as loss. But I was twenty and my father's death had been more complicated than that. Why, I wondered, was I telling Ramona about my father? I hardly ever talked about him. The bad motive was to gain her confidence. The good was that I felt comfortable in her presence. She was calm and matter-of-fact in her manner and answers. There was none of the jockeying for position that can happen with some women.

"Why did you want to know if I was married?" she asked.

"You have an Indian voice. You have an Anglo name."

"Franklin is my family name. We took it many years ago. My father was named Benjamin."

"Any guy who experimented with lightning is all right with me," I said.

"Sometimes when a crew sleeps on the mountain you will see lightning strike a tree and stand there and dance. She loved it when that happened. I have her boots in my backpack. The boots the hotshots get are custom-made to last, but she wore hers out. They rebuilt them, only the boots didn't fit after that and she gave them to me. I was wearing them that day. I can't wear them anymore. Would you give them to her mother and father for me?"

"Sure."

She opened her backpack and handed me a rolled-up brown bag. "Thanks. After the fire the Forest Service brought in people to help us 'deal with our grief,' they said. I said I wanted to deal with it my way, the Indian way. I went to the medicine man and told him I didn't know if I was a wigwam or a tepee. Do you know what

he said? 'Indian, your problem is that you are two tents.' "
She laughed.

I did, too. Some people get funnier when things get darker.

"That's a day fifteen joke," she said. "Sometimes hotshots are on a fire for twenty-one days before you get a day off, and you tell jokes so you don't go crazy. A joke that isn't funny on day one can be funny by day fifteen. By day twenty-one a really bad joke is very funny. Are you going to talk to Mike Marshall?"

"Tomorrow," I said.

"He knows some day twenty-one jokes."

If there was anything else to say, we weren't saying it. Ramona stared into space. Trying to avoid her eyes, I found myself staring into my empty cup. Silence fell like snowflakes across the table. "Well, thank you for your time," I said.

"It's nothing. Tell them I am very sorry for what happened."

"I will."

The bag Ramona had given me wasn't sealed, so when I got back to the office I opened it. Inside I found a pair of lace-up boots stained black from soot and white from sweat plus a manila envelope that had gotten sooty from the boots. The envelope wasn't sealed either and it didn't have anybody's name on it, so I opened that, too. It contained several photographs of firefighters wearing yellow shirts. The most interesting one to me was a woman who had to be Joni Barker standing alone in a clearing. She wore skintight Lycra running pants as torn and tattered as a pair of favorite jeans, and she had an enviable body— firm and fit. Joni had her mother's blond hair, pulled back into a ponytail, but a few curls had escaped and framed her face. She had on her firefighter boots, which was fortunate because the clearing she stood in was a nest of snakes. She had picked up two of them and held her arms up with the snakes curling down to her elbows.

I took the photo out to the reception area to show Anna. My former partner, Brink, had left Hamel & Harrison and gone into probate practice with his girlfriend, although I hadn't gotten around to taking his name off the door yet. Every once in a while I missed him, but not now, because I knew that whatever his reaction to the photo would be, it would be the wrong one. "What do you make of this?" I asked Anna. I needed to run it by someone; when it comes to snakes my reactions are too primal to be trusted.

"Who is she?" Anna asked.

"Joni Barker."

"Great bod!"

"She's the hotshot who died in the Thunder Mountain Fire."

"Wow!"

"She was a friend of Ramona Franklin, the woman I just had coffee with. Ramona's a Navajo, a firefighter, and a student at UNM. She was the lookout on the Thunder Mountain Fire but she says she didn't see anything. When I asked her if she thought the government screwed up, she said she didn't know."

"She probably needs the job."

"True." My gut reaction was to like and trust Ramona, my lawyer instinct is not to trust anyone. I started thinking like a lawyer and reconsidered what Ramona had said. Maybe she couldn't have seen the blowup from her station on the ridge. But "didn't" was the word she'd chosen. Carefully or randomly, who knew? Maybe she didn't look white people in the eye, maybe she didn't look lawyers in the eye, maybe she didn't look anybody in the eye. It could be the Indian way. It could be shyness. It could also be fear or guilt. These were calls I wasn't ready to make. But if we ever went to trial and she testified, her every glance and gesture would be open to interpretation—or misinterpretation—by a jury. It was more than possible there would be no lawsuit and no trial, that the blame between the lines would fall on the firefighters and not the bureaucrats, that my investigation would lead me to a situation more troubled than a nest of snakes.

"Why'd she give you the picture?" Anna asked.

"I'm not sure she was giving it to me. I found it in a package with Joni's boots."

Anna studied the picture. "You know, in sand paintings snakes represent lightning."

"I know."

"What do you think Joni's doing with the snakes in her arms? Praying for rain?"

"A firefighter is more likely to pray for lightning than for rain."

"Why?"

"That's where the jobs come from."

4

The next day I talked to Mike Marshall. He'd been house-sitting for a friend in Albuquerque and asked me to meet him there, which was all right with me. It's easier to know the truth about people when they're in their own environment surrounded by furniture that has their butt prints all over it. The house was near the university, on a street where the frame stucco houses had all been built at the same time. One ornery owner had turned his dwelling into a stainless-steel tower at the risk of pissing off the rest of the block. The other houses were all the same size and shape, set the same distance back from the curb. Streets where every building is evenly spaced make me feel like a crooked rat in a symmetrical maze. I prefer the randomness of my neighborhood.

But it didn't make much difference to Mike Marshall where he lived at this point. He was sheltered and that was about all he noticed. The shades of the house were drawn and the rooms were dark, but when he opened the door to let me in, the sunlight caught him. He was wearing shorts and a T-shirt. Fuzzy blond hair covered his arms and legs and the sunshine turned it golden. His eyes were an intense blue and speckled like a robin's egg. I guessed him to be twenty-six or -seven, a few years older than Joni.

"Come on in," he said.

We went into the living room. I sat down on the sofa, a wooden frame with a futon thrown over the back. Mike sat down on a metal chair at a table. "I talked to Ramona Franklin yesterday," I began.

"What'd she say?"

"Not much."

"Ramona's quiet."

"She has a sense of humor. She told me a day fifteen joke."

"I could use a day forty-five joke myself," he said.

"That's how long it's been?" For him it was the beginning of a long sentence with his heart in solitary lockup. Someday he'd be released, but he'd never be the same.

"Yeah. Ramona and Joni were good friends. Ramona's the point woman on the Duke City Hotshots. Some people resented her for that." A pad of paper and some colored pencils lay on the table. He picked up a green pencil, checked the tip, and began drawing on the paper.

"The point woman?"

"A crew boss gets points for hiring women and minorities. A woman who also happens to be Native American is worth a lot of points. It's not hard to find women firefighters, but it can be hard to find Native Americans because so many of the reservations have their own crews. It's good seasonal work. Some of the guys were bitter about Ramona getting hired, but she proved she can hang."

"She was the lookout at Thunder Mountain?"

"Right."

"She told me she didn't see the blaze."

"She's getting flack for that, but I was near the top of the north ridge and I didn't see it until it blew up either. The fire jumped the canyon and roared up the western slope. It sounded like a jet taking off." He stopped sketching for a minute and stared at his hands, which had the scabby look of burns healing.

"How did you escape?"

"I got into some good black and waited it out. Then I went over the ridge and walked out through the drainage on the other side. The black is the area on a fire that has already burned. It's the safest place to be, but a lot of the black at Thunder Mountain wasn't good because of the reburn potential of Gambel oak. Gambel oak has the ability to retain moisture. It may look like it has burned, but there can still be a lot of fuel left in a Gambel oak."

"You've read the report?"

"Yeah. It's a bunch of crap."

"It says that if the crew had dropped their packs they could have outrun the flames."

"That's a fucking lie. First of all, nobody drops their pack. Everything you need is inside. Your instinct is to hold on to it. The wind was forty miles an hour, the fire's rate of spread was eighteen miles an hour, the slope was sixty degrees, the flames were one hundred feet tall." Mike looked up at me as he rattled off his figures. He was very precise and sure of himself, and I was convinced. A narrow beam of sunlight had made its way through the closed curtains and across the room. It tapped Mike on the shoulder and he moved his chair to get away from it. "Fire moves faster uphill than down, people don't," he said. "The firefighters are also getting criticized for not deploying their shelters. You read that, too?"

"Yeah."

"Nobody is going to take the time to drop their pack or get into their shake-and-bake when a fire is breathing down their neck. The pucker factor is too high. Your instinct is to run, but there's no way anybody could have outrun that blaze. It blew up too fast and hot. The heat killed the hotshots before the fire did. It seared their lungs. Now the Forest Service and the BLM are trying to cover their asses. It's easy to blame the hotshots; they're dead.

"But the really bad decisions were made higher up. They're criticizing Ramona because she didn't see the blowup, but where the hell was the aerial surveillance? The Forest Service's own meteorologist knew the cold front was moving in, but they never told us. We were getting our weather reports from the weather channel. Many of the hotshots had never fought a Gambel oak fire before. We were helicoptered to Thunder Mountain in the morning with no briefing. A couple of years ago there was a Gambel oak fire in Lone Ridge, Colorado. The crew boss, who'd lost three of his crew on that fire, prepared a report on the special properties of Gambel oak, but the Forest Service stuck it on a shelf and never showed it to a single firefighter. These were situations that shout watch out, but the Forest Service ignored them." He picked up his pencil again and began moving it across the page with a quick, sharp motion.

"Why did the Forest Service ignore the dangers of the situation?"

"Because too many fires were burning then and resources were stretched thin. Because people are moving near wilderness areas and they expect the government to protect their houses. Because a homeowner will bitch to a congressman, but a tree won't. Nobody's house is worth risking a firefighter's life for. Nobody's. If this goes to court and you need somebody to testify for you, I'll do it."

"Thanks," I said. Mike also had poetry in his speech. I guess that's what you'd expect from a job that deals with life and death. He was articulate and angry, a mixture of precision and passion. The ability to reel off facts and numbers would make him a good witness for me, maybe even an expert witness, but the government's lawyer would be likely to poke at the cinders of his anger until they exploded.

"This case may never go to court; Eric doesn't want to sue. He feels that conditions were so bad that day that what happened was unavoidable."

"Yeah, well, it makes it easier for him to accept Joni's death if he thinks it was an act of God. But he was a firefighter and he knows better. He'll change his mind when he gets to the site. A lot of firefighters don't want to get involved because they're afraid of losing their jobs. Me, I've got nothing to lose. I'm not going back on the line anyway. I'd be too cautious now to be any good."

"What are you going to do?"

"Go back to school." I could see the appeal of academia to someone who'd been through what he had.

"Computers?" He had the mind for it.

"Engineering."

"Ramona gave me Joni's boots and some pictures of the hotshots. She asked me to pass them on to the Barkers," I said.

"Is the picture with the snakes in there?"

"Yeah."

"I'd give them the other stuff but not that picture. It makes people uneasy. We were on a trail crew that day. Joni saw the snakes and waded in. A lot of guys on the crew wouldn't have done that. She was a strong woman. I would have trusted my life with her. I did trust my life to her, and to Ramona, too." His hand was sliding across the page, filling in the blanks, maybe, of what he'd already done.

"Nancy Barker seems to want to avoid Ramona. Do you know why?"

He shrugged. "It could be because Ramona survived the fire and Joni didn't. Maybe she's blaming Ramona, but she shouldn't."

"Do you want the picture of Joni?" I asked. "If you don't, I might like to keep it until this case is settled."

"Keep it," he said. "I've got plenty of pictures of Joni."

"What was she like?"

"Joni? She was full of life, full of fun. She loved fire fighting."

"What did she love about it?"

"The excitement, the danger, the adrenaline rush. Fire-fighters are basically adrenaline junkies. Joni was very strong and athletic. We were mogul skiers in the winter. Did you know that?"

"No."

"I've got a video here of us skiing last winter at Breckenridge. Would you like to see it? It'll give you a feeling for the kind of person Joni was."

"Okay," I said.

He got up and pulled the curtains tighter, blocking out the rogue ray of sunshine that had annoyed him. He inserted the video and the TV turned the brilliant blue of a western sky until the screen filled with the whiteness of snow. After I stared at it for a minute, bumps took shape and I could see that it was a field of moguls. Mike would probably know the exact pitch of the slope; all I knew was that it was elevator-shaft steep. The video was being shot from the chairlift. Two specks showed up at the top of the screen and began maneuvering their way down the mountain while the camera moved toward them. Mike plowed through the moguls with his head down and his shoulders hunched, strong, steady, determined as a buffalo. Joni was an antelope: light, graceful, joy in motion. She careened off the moguls and got to the bottom a few seconds ahead of Mike.

A camera at the bottom of the hill closed in on them. Mike had bent over and was adjusting something on his boot. Joni took off her helmet, shook her blond hair loose, and smiled triumphantly for the world and the camera. They were far from the grubbiness of fire, but not that far from the spirit of fire fighting. Adrenaline is adrenaline. Power is power. The younger and more promising the person, the sadder the death, but some deaths go beyond sadness into the tragedy realm. Joni must have had faults. She might have been mean, irritable, or arrogant, but she'd had the kind of radiance that could turn her life into legend and her death into myth. People would be remembering Joni Barker and the Duke City Hotshots for a long, long time.

Mike was staring at his pad and tears were watering his scorched hands. I got up, took the remote from the table, and snapped the video off. When I reached over his shoulder to grab the remote, I saw that the pad he'd been drawing on contained graph paper. On a page divided into tiny squares, he'd been drawing trees: deciduous trees, evergreen trees, standing trees, fallen trees. His voice became husky. "Get the assholes who were responsible for this," he said.

"I'll try." I went back to my seat on the sofa with the remote still in my hand. I wanted a cigarette, but I was in a no-smoking household. I'd known that the minute I stepped in the door. "I used to be a skier," I told Mike.

"You skied?" he asked.

"Yup," I said.

He blew his nose. "That's a surprise. I mean, well, you don't look like an athlete."

What did I look like? A smoker and a drinker? A lawyer who was pushing forty? I had been an athlete. I'd been a die-hard skier, in fact, but even then I smoked and drank, stayed up all night and smoked joints in the chairlift, getting by on adrenaline rather than healthy habits. You can do that when you're twenty. "I grew up in the East. I ski-bummed in New England." I skied on rocks and mud. I skied on glare ice and black ice, mashed potatoes, corn snow, and slush. I skied in rain and sleet and occasionally even snow and sun. I skied when it was fifteen degrees below zero and my skin was turning to frost.

"I'm a Western skier," Mike said. But he'd skied like an Easterner, tight and controlled, relying on technique, where Joni had relied on reflexes and grace.

I'd perfected my own technique until I forgot I had one, until my turns had a quick and easy flow. One day I had a perfect run under a deep blue sky in six inches of new powder, and I never skied again. Would Mike quit skiing now? I wondered. "You know the rush you get when you're skiing the fall line at the edge of your ability?" I asked him.

"Yeah."

"Fire fighting must be like that."

"It is. You get in the zone. All the training kicks in and you go on automatic. You look up and the day is over."

"You're pursuing a risky activity with people you care about. The feeling of camaraderie must be similar."

"It's very strong. When the wind is right I'm going back to Thunder Mountain. The Forest Service agreed to helicopter the families in. I can prove there's no way Joni could have escaped that fire even if she had dropped her pack or deployed her shelter, and I'm going to do it. They're not going to get away with blaming her for this. Do you want to come?"

"Yeah," I said.

5

We couldn't go on any ordinary day. It had to be a day
that approximated the conditions of the fatal fire when
the winds howled out of the South Canyon like a terrible red wolf and moved faster than a bird could fly. But
the winds, which didn't want to stop in June, wouldn't
return in August. At first I watched the weather forecast
every night, waiting for the winds to pick up and for the
Barkers to call, but then I stopped thinking about the
Thunder Mountain Fire. Real estate and divorce were
how I made my living. The Thunder Mountain suit had
a lot of potential but it also had some major strikes
against it. Feuding clients wasn't the only one. Negligence and personal responsibility are complex issues. I
wasn't an ambulance chaser and I wasn't sure I wanted
to be a liability lawyer either. Three weeks later when
the winds finally rose I didn't notice; Mike's phone call
came as a surprise.

"High winds tomorrow," he said. "And we're going to Thunder Mountain. Wanna come?"

Yes, but could I rearrange my schedule to fit it in? I looked at my calendar. Nothing there that couldn't wait. "Okay," I said.

"The Forest Service helicopter will pick you and the Barkers up at Kirtland at oh-nine hundred."

"Where do we meet you?"

"The parking lot at the campground near the foot of Thunder Mountain. That was the loading field for the fire. Ramona and I are driving up together. The Forest Service's P.R. guy, Tom Hogue, will come with you and the Barkers. He's a smoke."

"A smoke?"

"An asshole. He resents having women in the Forest Service and he's just putting in time until he retires. I don't want to spend any more time with that guy than I have to."

And maybe Ramona was going with Mike because she didn't want to spend any more time with the Barkers than she had to. "See you at Thunder Mountain," I said.

Eric and Nancy Barker were dressed for climbing in hiking shorts, T-shirts with green ribbons over their hearts, and matching bandannas. Eric carried a large backpack. His sunglasses were balanced on top of his head, staring at the sky. They both had the strong calf muscles of serious hikers. Hogue was dressed in a green Forest Service uniform. I wore jeans and running shoes myself, and carried my Aunt Joan's birding binoculars.

Hogue and the Barkers were standing near the helicopter when I got to the airfield. Hogue saw me coming and glanced at his watch. What's this guy's problem? I wondered. I worked fifteen minutes from Kirtland. How late could I have been?

"Traffic," I said, and was pissed at myself for having said anything at all. "I'm Neil Hamel."

"Tom Hogue." He was tall and thin with a white mustache that made his face look as if it had been brushed by frost. The chopper blade spun impatiently, but Hogue had some things to say first.

"Mike Marshall and Ramona Franklin are meeting us in the parking lot, correct?" he shouted.

"Yes," Eric replied.

"I've arranged for the helicopter to come back for us at three. Will that present a problem for anyone?"

"Not for us," Nancy said.

"Me neither," I said.

"I've made several of these trips," Hogue said. "I feel its necessary to warn you that it can be difficult emotionally and physically."

"We'll manage," Eric said.

"All right then. Let's get going." Hogue took a remote out of his pocket and clicked it next to each of his ears. He wore a hearing aid, I figured. This was his way of controlling the input and lowering the volume. If Hogue was the Forest Service's P.R. man I wouldn't want to meet their axman. On the other hand, it couldn't be easy to return to the fire scene time after time with grieving and angry parents.

Hogue motioned us inside the aircraft. We sat down and the chopper lifted off. This helicopter was used to carrying a larger load. There was plenty of space inside and Hogue sat down several feet from the Barkers and me.

While we lifted off I studied him. There wasn't much else to look at. Hogue struck me as a guy who'd been single for a long time. Maybe he'd been married once, maybe it didn't take. Guys who are long-term single seem to be surrounded by an invisible bubble. Single women could well have their own bubbles, but I'm not the one to notice that. I saw Hogue's bubble as hard, transparent, cold. Inside he'd keep the attitudes he wanted to protect, outside were the ones he'd prefer to ignore. A remote, older man appeals to a lot of women, but I have a built-in ice detector. I know that with a guy like that you can chop away with your ice pick forever and never get through.

Once we were in the air I turned my eyes away from Hogue and toward the ground. A lot of things are revealed from the air, and pilots are the ones to see them. The year I was a ski bum I knew a pilot who buzzed the town every morning to find out where his buddies had spent the night.

Our helicopter whirred over Sandia Indian Bingo, whose full parking lot was a stark contrast to the emptiness of the rest of the reservation. We followed the green thread of the Rio Grande Valley for a while, then crossed over Los Alamos and Abiquiu Dam. We flew over the Jicarilla Apache Reservation, and I spotted the blue jewels of Heron and El Vado lakes. The Carson National Forest was down below, and it was reassuring to see how much of it remained green. The Barkers sat together hip to hip and didn't say a word. It was difficult to communicate above the noise of the helicopter anyway.

It was obvious the minute we crossed the Colorado border. I saw long lines of condominium roofs and houses surrounded by acres of fields or backed up against the wilderness. Some were trophy sized, some were tiny hunting cabins, but those were remnants of a poorer era. Baja Colorado (lower Colorado) is a phrase you hear in New Mexico once developers start showing up. We have pockets of development among our mountains and deserts—ranchettes in the East Mountains, sprawl on the West Mesa, Santa Fe's million-dollar casitas—but you have to cross the border into Colorado and Arizona to find development big time. That's when I realize how close to the Third World the Land of Enchantment is. Once you cross the state line, "For Sale" signs sprout like weeds beside the highway. In southern Colorado everything seems to have a price; in New Mexico we still have the original Spanish land grants, where signs say that nothing is for sale ever.

The helicopter began its descent and Nancy gripped Eric's hand. Our range of vision became more limited and more precise. Cars and trucks rode a highway and beside it a brown ribbon of a river flowed. We crossed a valley where horses grazed. There were a couple of A-frames and a log cabin in the valley. People here must have gone about their business while the fire raged several miles away. We were approaching Thunder Mountain. The piñon and juniper on its western slope churned like surf in the wind. The chopper crossed a ridge and we were looking into the heart of devastation. Hogue fumbled with his remote and cleared his throat. Nancy buried her face in her hands. Eric pulled his dark glasses down.

The ground was the color of pink skin. Tree trunks were black stubble on a face that had been scraped raw. The steep walls of the South Canyon were burned bare. There was a dry arroyo at the bottom, but often it was hidden by the shape of the canyon walls. I could understand how a lookout on the ridge might miss a fire in the arroyo, though from the air it should have been easy enough to spot the smoke.

The pilot negotiated the chopper through the high winds. We passed the helipad at the top of the ridge, the place the hotshots had been dropped in, the place from which their bodies had to be lifted out, the place we would return to once we had picked up Mike and Ramona.

"I don't think I can go down there, Eric." The pain in Nancy's voice cut through the roar of the chopper. "You go if you want to. I'll wait below." Eric squeezed her hand and said nothing.

We descended along the eastern slope, which was as heavily forested as the western slope had been except for some dark patches where the fire had spotted. I could see a serpentine dirt road curving up the far side of this canyon. About halfway up stood a massive wooden house with a cedar-shake roof. It was clear from here how close this trophy had come to being kindling. Standing on the deck watching the smoke rise, who wouldn't have reached for the phone and called anyone with influence?

The pilot negotiated the parking lot landing. Mike was visible waiting next to a red car, but there was no sign of Ramona. We landed, escaped for a minute from the noise of the whirling bird, and went to talk to Mike. He gave Nancy and Eric an awkward hug. He carried a large backpack and a radio, and wore a green hard hat, wool pants, a bumble-bee yellow shirt with long sleeves, and a red bandanna around his neck. It had to be an uncomfortably hot outfit, and we were a long way from a live fire. It must have been the same outfit he and Joni were wearing the day she died.

"Where's Ramona?" Eric asked.

"She's hiking in. She wanted to face the mountain in her own way," Mike said.

"That's the way Ramona does everything, isn't it? Her own way." Nancy looked across the canyon to where the trophy house was making a loud statement. "My daughter died trying to save that house," she cried, shaking like an aspen in the strong wind.

"Come here, Nancy," Eric said. He took her hand and they walked to the edge of the parking lot, where they stood under the shade of a large cottonwood. He'd hitched up his pack, and red sticks that resembled dynamite were sticking out of it. The Barkers appeared to be engaged in the mixture of negotiation, argument, and understanding that comes with a long-term relationship. The arms of a cottonwood are a good place to hide and think. Tom Hogue watched them from where he stood near the helicopter. Mike and I were far enough away from the noise that we could talk without shouting.

"Disappearing into the shade of a tree is a firefighter's trick," Mike said. "You'd be amazed how many firefighters can hide under the shade of one tree."

"That gear you're wearing looks *muy* hot," I said.

"After a while you hardly notice. How do you like my pants?"

"They're okay."

"They're women's. All the guys bitched when they started making special pants for the women, but one by one they started wearing them."

"Why?"

"Better fit. They've got more room. Joni used to joke about my getting into her pants." The wind danced a dust devil around the parking lot. Mike looked up the mountain at the rippling piñon and juniper. "I'd like to get going. The updrafts increase at this time of day."

"This is the time of the fire?"

"Getting close. The sky was like this then, so clear and blue that everybody miscalculated the strength of the cold front that was moving in."

I was curious about the absent Ramona. "Would a Navajo woman go back to the place where someone she cared for died? Navajos are known to be suspicious about death."

"She'll have to make her own decision about that when she gets nearby. She wants to leave a tribute to Joni somewhere on the mountain. The Native American firefighters like to leave something at a fire. She didn't have a chance to do it before."

"When did she leave here?"

"About an hour ago."

"Will she meet us on the mountain?"

"That's up to her. You guys ready?" Mike yelled at Eric and Nancy. Nancy shook her head, sat down, and leaned against the tree. Eric walked over to us, and then so did Hogue, who was clicking on his hearing aid and looking at his watch.

"She doesn't want to go?" Hogue asked Eric.

"No."

"The mothers never do," he said. "Where's Ramona Franklin? We can't wait here for her all day."

"You don't have to wait for Ramona. She's already on the mountain," Mike answered.

"I don't want to leave Nancy here alone," Eric said. "You guys go, let us know everything you see. Okay?" He punched Mike's shoulder lightly with his fist.

"Will do," Mike said.

6

In the helicopter Mike and Hogue tried to ignore each other, but their body language indicated they were all too aware. From this side of the mountain the burned area looked like a pink conch shell floating on a green sea. The pilot dropped us off at the helipad. The helicopter was creating its own weather system, a tempest within the cold front. The sky was a calm, deep blue, but the winds were churning on top of the ridge and the temperature felt fifteen degrees cooler than it had below. Hogue told the pilot that he was thinking about walking out and having someone from the Forest Service pick him up in the parking lot later; he wanted to check the condition of the forest on the east side of the mountain. The pilot confirmed that he would come back for Mike and me at three.

The South Canyon looked even more desolate up close than it had from the air. The devastation was absolute. Downed trees, twisted by fire, resembled black lizards crawling over the canyon walls. The remaining trees had burned down to stumps. At my feet lay a handful of empty, white snail shells. The only signs of life I noticed in the canyon came from the base of the Gambel oaks, where pale green leaves sprouted. The restless wind seemed hell-bent on making it to Kansas for dinner; then it spun around and whipped the loose pink soil into billowing shapes of clouds and flame. Hogue clicked his remote near his right ear, then his left, turning down the wind's volume. I could see why; I was hearing voices in the wind.

"Was the wind this squirrelly the day of the fire?" I asked Mike.

"Worse," he said.

"I'm smelling something burning or burnt. Could it be the fire after all this time?"

"Could be. Yellowstone smelled for months. I've lost my sense of smell myself. I've eaten too much smoke. I'll be coughing up black stuff until November." He looked across the canyon to a spot near the top of the opposite ridge. "That was where I escaped to. It was good black PJ—that's what we call piñon, juniper—and it didn't burn again. But down below there was more Gambel oak. The fire was in the drainage, then it started up this side. That's where it blew up, jumped the canyon, and trapped the firefighters." He pointed to a line of white crosses climbing the slope that resembled stitches on the naked hill. Each one marked a place where a firefighter had fallen and died. "The hotshots had been coming back up. The blowup took them by surprise. They weren't as concerned as they should have been because the area they were in had burned previously. They didn't know about the reburn potential of Gambel oak." Mike turned hard eyes toward Hogue, who busied himself with his radio.

The wind blew into our faces and covered us with a layer of pink dust that clung to everything but the bristles on Hogue's white mustache. When the dust settled I could see a rectangle carved into the slope to the left of the crosses. I peered through my Aunt Joan's birding binoculars and focused on the rectangle that had been formed by four burned logs. Inside a stick figure made from pink stones was wearing a hard hat and running.

Mike saw where I was looking. "The firefighters left that monument. Makes a statement, doesn't it?"

"Yeah," I said. Someday something slick and smooth would be erected here, but it would never have the power of this crude, raw box.

Mike hitched up his pack, turned around, and looked at the opposite ridge. Red sticks were attached to the sides of his pack and bottles of oil dangled from the bottom. He pointed at a spot near the middle of the saddle. "That's where Ramona was."

I looked down into the drainage, trying to visualize what Ramona could or could not have seen. Even without the trees there were so many ridges and gullies in the South Canyon that there didn't seem to be anyplace you could see all of it at once.

Hogue cleared his throat. "Actually, the interagency report placed Ramona Franklin about fifty yards south."

"That's bullshit," Mike said. "Her post was exactly where I said it was."

"Where is she anyway?" Hogue asked, glancing around the naked canyon. "Isn't she supposed to be meeting us here?"

"She's coming," Mike said.

Hogue looked at his watch. "When? Indian time?"

"I said she was coming."

"If she thinks the report misrepresented her position this is her chance to explain," Hogue said.

"She's not going to say anything in front of you but 'Yes, sir,'" Mike answered. "She's got a kid. She needs the money. She needs the job. You can take if from me, that was Ramona's post, that's where she was assigned, and that's where she stood."

"Why wasn't she on her radio? No one mentioned hearing her in the report."

"She didn't have anything to say."

"There was talk she programmed her radio to the wrong frequency."

"Ramona knows how to program a radio. The problem with this fire wasn't that Ramona couldn't see it. The problem was that there was no aerial surveillance."

We were near the ridge top and it was hard to maintain your balance in the strong wind. Hogue was digging in his heels. "That wasn't the only problem," he said. "The hotshots were constructing fireline downhill. They didn't drop their backpacks when threatened. They didn't deploy their fire shelters. Those are three situations right there that shout watch out. It's all in the interagency report."

"You know what you can do with your interagency report ... You can take your ..." Mike hitched up his backpack, giving him the hunched shoulder silhouette of a mountain goat. He leaned forward as if intending to butt Hogue's head, but he stopped himself, saying, "Never mind." He began striding downhill.

Hogue stared at Mike's retreating back. "The Forest Service sure isn't what it used to be," he said. I didn't particularly feel like hanging around Hogue reminiscing about the good old days, so I followed Mike down the precipitous slope, feeling the earth crumble beneath my feet. It was dust now, but one day rain would turn this hill into a mud slide. My knees hurt from holding the rest of me in check. Climbing hurts your knees when you go down and your lungs when you go up. Mike stopped about halfway down and stared across the narrow drainage at the row of white crosses. When I caught up, his eyes were tearing from the wind and the pain. "Joni is the number-seven cross," he said. He shook himself and channeled the pain into measuring the natural forces. "That slope is sixty degrees. The wind was forty miles an hour the day of the fire. It's thirty-five today."

"How can you tell?" I asked.

"Experience."

He sounded convincing to me, and Hogue, who had climbed down to where we stood, didn't challenge him.

"See that spot?" Mike pointed to a place beneath the crosses where the fallen trees were thicker.

"Yeah."

"That's where the fire jumped the drainage. In order to

escape it the hotshots would have had to run over six hundred yards in a minute. It wouldn't have made any difference whether they carried their packs or dropped them and stripped naked. No one can run that fast on a sixty-degree slope. It can't be done and I'm going to prove it. Joni could sprint one hundred yards in fifteen seconds. I can do it in ten. He handed me a stopwatch. "I'm going to run the distance with and without my pack. Will you time me?"

"Sure."

"Okay, let's do it."

The crosses were a short distance away as the bird flies or the fire jumps, but getting to them was a steep and difficult climb down to the drainage and back up the other side. Mike did it faster than Hogue and me. When we caught up, he had taken a rose from his backpack and placed it at the foot of Joni's cross. Several of the other crosses were marked by ribbons and flowers.

"I'm going to start at the place where the fire jumped the drainage," he said. "Time me to the top cross. That's two hundred and fifty yards."

"Okay," I said.

He ran the distance first with the pack and then without. Each time he began with a fierce burst of speed but slowed down as he ascended the slope. Even without the pucker factor he seemed to be running as hard as anyone could. It took him four minutes to run the distance with the pack. Three and a half without. He came over to me when he had finished, but he was still in the zone. His eyes had a look of glazed ferocity and total concentration. Hogue saw it and moved further up the slope.

"Mike?" I said.

He shook his head and came back to the present. "How'd I do?"

"Thirty seconds faster without the pack."

He did some mental calculations. "I was right," he said. "No way she could have made it out of here with or without the pack."

"Does it help to know that?"

"It proves they were wrong. It proves they had no right to criticize her in their report. Joni knew what she was doing." He put his hand on her cross. "That was for you, babe," he said. "And now I gotta get out of here." He shouldered his pack, wiped his eyes, and began climbing uphill.

Hogue was standing near the second cross from the top. "This is where Chancellor's ax was found," he said when Mike reached him.

"So?" replied Mike.

"His body was found in the number-nine position."

"I know that," Mike snapped. Hogue was an annoying mosquito who didn't know when to buzz off. Mike was a person who didn't want to be bugged. Tension was building in the narrow canyon.

"He must have dropped his pack and gone back to help the women out."

"Chancellor didn't drop his pack. When the flames hit him they burned the ax off." Mike spoke slowly, leaving spaces between the words as if he were talking to a child or a jury. "The women on this crew were hotshots who were dropped into a red-flag situation. They didn't need

Chancellor's help. They needed the support of the Forest Service. They needed a fire supervisor who knew what the hell he was doing."

"If the flames hit Chancellor here, then why was his body found in the number-nine position?" Hogue asked.

"He was on fire at that point. He was already dead. He didn't know what he was doing. He just ran." Mike's words came closer together now. His patience was running out.

Hogue's response was a shrug—a stupid, annoying gesture. Maybe he didn't know any better, maybe he couldn't help himself. This situation seemed to be taking on its own momentum and spiraling out of control. The death and the tension in the canyon were bringing out the beast in everyone. The conditions were ripe, the wind was up. Mike was about to explode and there wasn't anything I could do to stop him. In a way it was a relief when the blowup came.

"You're a pain in the ass, you know that!" Mike shouted.

Hogue's response was to tighten his lips. "That's insubordination," he answered. "It'll cost you your job."

Mike grabbed Hogue by his lapels. "As far as I'm concerned you can shove your fucking job. I'm out of the Forest Service." Mike was in Hogue's face. His hair was electric. His eyes were wild.

The eye in the calm of the storm was Hogue's unruffled contempt. "This is what happens when you hire people based on their gender or color instead of their ability." There were no more secrets on this naked hill. It was all coming out: the meanness, the prejudice, the anger, the power. "If you ever find Ramona Franklin on this mountain you can tell her she's out of the Forest Service, too." Hogue's narrow eyes indicated he was mean enough to do it.

"You son of a bitch," Mike said. He dropped Hogue's lapels and stomped up the mountain, leaving deep imprints in the soft soil and me alone with Tom Hogue.

7

Mike was over the ridge long before we got there. With or without the anger factor it was a long, steep climb. Hogue paused occasionally, waiting for me to catch up. The altitude was turning my heart into an engine running on low-octane gas. I felt that even if I could suck up every bit of oxygen in the South Canyon, it wouldn't be enough.

"I don't enjoy this sort of thing much anymore," Hogue said at one point.

Did he mean the hiking, I wondered, the fighting, or the firefighters who'd fallen on this hill?

"The Forest Service isn't what it used to be." He'd already said that. "Everybody wants a piece of the forest these days: the loggers, the spotted owl lovers, the ranchers, the environmentalists. I'm looking forward to retirement."

"Right," I replied. Women had invaded the old boy network. They shouldered the saws and jumped from the planes and were working their way up in management. If Hogue stuck around long enough he might even get one for a boss, and she could make it harder for him to fire a point woman (or anybody else) in an angry fit. But catching my breath seemed more important than wasting any more of it on him.

When we reached the helipad Hogue looked at his watch. "Only two-ten," he said, but we could already hear the helicopter buzzing across the valley.

He got the pilot on the radio. "There's a fire burning at Crested Butte. I'm on my way up there," the pilot squawked. "You guys still need me to pick you up?"

"Mike Marshall took off. I'm planning on walking myself, but I've got a lady here who seems a little tired."

"I'm not *that* tired," I said.

"It's a strenuous hike. You sure you're up to it?"

"I'm up to it."

"Okay," said Hogue, getting back on the radio. "Go on up to Crested Butte. We're walking."

Hogue and I started down the wooded side of the mountain. By now Mike could already be near the parking lot. He'd know the way out; he'd done it before. But there really was only one way—down. Ramona could be waiting for him at the car, or she could be anywhere else on the mountain, leaving her tribute. It would be easy enough to lose a person in the PJ forest. All I could see was the juniper in front of me, the piñon behind, the Gambel oak clustered everywhere—and all of it taller than I was. Hogue had gone on ahead but it didn't matter; he wasn't my idea of a great traveling companion. The forest wasn't as lush as it had appeared from the air. There were places where the fire had spotted, where cinders had jumped the ridge. I didn't see any fallen trees, but some of the trunks were charred black and the smell of the burn seemed even stronger over here.

Hogue waited for me at the top of a side ridge, one of the few places on the mountain where you could get a clear view of the canyon. We stopped and took a long drink of water from the bottle in his backpack. The wind seemed to have died down. At least it wasn't turning me into a big-haired woman or blowing dust in my face.

"How'd you finally get the fire out?" I asked Hogue.

"Bucket drops, slurry," he said.

Across the drainage, snuggled among the piñon, juniper, and Gambel oak, was the trophy house I'd seen from the air. It was the size of a destination resort. From here I could also see into the parking lot at the trailhead. Mike's car was there, but I didn't see Mike, Ramona, or the Barkers. North of the parking lot a dusty cloud hovered over the drainage area like a smoke signal that had run out of lift. The winds had slowed down enough to hold it in place.

"Is that smoke?" I asked Hogue.

"Dust," he replied. "It's a false smoke. There's a road down there. Kicks up a lot of dust this time of year."

We kept on trekking. The eastern slope was as precipitous as the western slope had been, and the going was slow. My toes slammed into the fronts of my running shoes and were turning numb. It felt like the beginning of frostbite. To the north of us I could see an area where the fire had leaped the ridge and burned about a third of the way down, about as far down as we'd come. I began making narrow traverses to cut the steepness, wishing I had a pair of custom-made hotshot boots, remembering a pair of favorite ski boots. It would have been a challenge to ski this slope if I were in shape and if I still skied. When I skied we used to joke about making birch christies, grabbing a tree and swinging yourself around it when you got into trouble. I grabbed a juniper to catch my breath and got a handful of pine tar.

The smell of smoke was stronger. The wind had returned with a vengeance. The afternoon updrafts were whipping the PJ into a jittery dance. The air seemed charged with nervous electricity. I came to a hump in the hill and there, as I'd always known someday it would be, was death staring me in the face. Hogue had seen it, and he turned toward me with the expression of stark terror you see on an unwrapped mummy. Death was behind him and it was the fire this time. Nothing false about the smoke we saw now. The smoke I'd been smelling hadn't been an illusion or the ghost of fire past. A monstrous orange glow filled the drainage. I looked into it and saw bursts of dazzling yellow as trees candled out, fire within the blaze. How had it gotten so big so fast? I wondered. High winds and fuel buildup had to be the answer. The trees that had hidden it before were fueling it now. There was a sudden roar like an F-16 taking off, the hiss of Gambel oaks giving up their lives. The heat became intense and seemed to zap the fluids from my body. Fingers of flame explored the side ridges to the north and the south. Directly in front of us the fire blew up to the size of downtown. It was still a couple of city blocks away, but moving fast, a lot faster than I could even with a major pucker factor. For a moment I couldn't move at all. I was an icicle in the face of the flames, frozen in place. My first thought was of the Kid. My second was of my house. My third was that I wanted to get the hell out of there.

"Run," Hogue screamed.

"Where?"

"To the black."

He turned and raced up the mountain, pursuing a course diagonal to the fire. I followed. If I'd had a pack I doubt I'd have had the time or wits to unload it. My instinct was to turn my back to the fire, go for distance, and run straight up, but fire, I knew, moves faster uphill than people can. I followed Hogue. The flames crackled and hissed below us. The fire was a hot, hungry dragon and we were its food. My shadow extended uphill and became a monster in the fire's glow.

The black had been visible from the side ridge, but here I couldn't see it because of the trees. Until the trees in front of us burned up we couldn't see how near we were to the black, and once that happened we'd be a part of the black ourselves. I had no way of pacing myself. I just ran as fast and hard as I could. I ran until I was gagging and coughing. I ran until whatever moisture I had left had sizzled out of me.

The fire's hot breath was scorching my back when I saw some black tree trunks ahead. Hogue dove into them and I followed, hoping this was real black, good black, black without the potential to reburn. The fire roared and made a run on our left, consuming the PJ with voracious appetite and speed. It nibbled at the edge of the black, but found nothing to feed on. It burned the PJ with an intense red heat, leaving behind a blinding cloud of smoke. I'd skied in a whiteout once where I couldn't see my hands or feet, didn't know if I was going up or down, didn't know where anybody else on the slope was, and kept calling out so I wouldn't bump into them. Hogue was in here somewhere, but I couldn't hear or see him. "Hogue," I yelled, but he didn't answer. There were tree trunks in the black, but I couldn't see them either until I collided with one. My forehead smacked into a trunk. My ears were ringing, my eyes were stinging and tearing, my face was bleeding from the tree I'd hit. I was eating, drinking, sweating, and coughing up smoke. Death by smoke inhalation was making death by fire look downright appealing. At least fire was quick. I was desperate to escape from the heat and the smoke. I had an all-consuming thirst that only an IV could fill. I felt nauseous and dizzy, so I got down on my hands and knees and vomited smoke. "Help," I called until my voice became a pathetic croak. There was some sort of answer, but my brain wasn't able to process it. "Here," I gagged.

There's a place where heat turns to cold, fire to ice, legal business to dreams, and that's where I was headed. In the lore of ice and snow there's always the story of an explorer or skier who becomes crazed by the cold, thinks she's burning up and throws her clothes off. That the opposite could occur in fire was my last thought before I entered the kingdom of snow and came out on a perfect winter day, crisp, clear, freezing. Cold bit my nose and I could see the shape of my breath. The air was clear, but so cold it hurt to breathe. The only way to get warm was to ski fast and hard. The sky was as blue as it ever gets in the East. The snow sparkled like Ivory flakes. There were six inches of new powder, and I was skiing the Rumble alone. It was a side trail where no one could see me, but that didn't matter; I wasn't performing for anybody on the lift. I was out here for Joe and myself, skiing the fall line in linked turns. The snow came over the top of my boots; all I could see of my skis in the fresh powder was the tips. The turns flowed into one another, smooth, quick, easy. I only had to flex my ankles and shift my weight. I was in the zone, queen of the hill, master of my sport. The pain that Joe wasn't alive to enjoy it was the long shadow I was trailing, but if I skied fast enough I could stay ahead of it. I looked down and saw him waiting for me at the bottom of the Rumble. He was wearing a plaid jacket and smoking a cigarette. The smoke expanded, slipping through the trees, billowing, smothering, making me gag and cough.

A voice brought me back to the harsher reality of heat and smoke. "You will be all right," it said. "This is good black. It won't reburn. The fire cannot reach you here. I'll wrap you in this to keep the heat off and the smoke out. Stay inside. I will come back for you when the danger is over."

It was a cocoon, a space blanket, a fire shelter. The arms that wrapped me in it were firm and strong. The voice I heard belonged to a woman.

8

When I woke up I was still seeing white, not the blinding white of snowfall or the searing white of smoke but the antiseptic white of a hospital room. A nurse was adjusting the IV I'd been craving. A stern and fit doctor came in to tell me I was suffering from smoke inhalation and dehydration and that he wanted to keep me in the hospital for a few days for observation. I looked up at the dull white ceiling, heard the woman in the next bed gag and throw up, listened to the clatter of food trays in the hallway, and decided that if I was going to be sick I wanted to do it in my own bed, looking at my skylight, listening to the sounds my house made. When I told the doctor I didn't have any insurance, he said he'd consider releasing me the next day.

As soon as the doctor departed an investigator for the Forest Service entered and sat down in a chair beside my bed. His name, he said, was Henry Ortega. He had a long face and a mustache that nestled above his lip like a large, brown moth.

"We're very glad you are going to be all right." He sighed.

I answered with a gut-wrenching cough that seemed as if it would last into the next millennium.

"I know how you feel," he said. "I was on the line for ten years and every season I coughed up smoke until Thanksgiving. You were very lucky that Ramona Franklin was on the mountain and carrying her equipment. She found you, wrapped a wet bandanna around your face, and covered you with her fire shelter."

"That was Ramona who spoke to me?"

"Must have been. Once the fire was extinguished and the smoke died down, a helicopter lifted you out. I thought you would like this." He presented me with the fire shelter, a crinkly mess of Mylar that probably resembled the surface of my lungs. I knew where it would end up—in the closet of the empty room. Maybe I'd take it out someday if I needed reminding of how close I'd been to becoming a crispy critter. Maybe not.

"Thanks," I said. My voice was the rasp of someone who'd smoked for two lifetimes or spent one day on the fireline. If I hadn't had any respect for the endurance of firefighters before, I did now. "What happened to Ramona? Did she get out all right?"

Henry nodded. "She had to leave you to save herself. She managed to escape over the ridge into the South Canyon. We found her there, shaking and crying." Willingly or not Ramona had ended up near the place where

Joni had died. "She's been through a lot." Henry Ortega's eyes were deep and soulful. Another poet whose profession happened to be fire. "The hospital examined and released her. We offered her counseling with a trained professional, but she refused."

"Ramona does things her own way. Is she here? Can I talk to her?"

"She's been released."

"What happened to Tom Hogue?"

Henry Ortega looked at his hands, studying the fingernails and knuckles that had been outlined by ten years of soot. "He was found dead on the mountain."

"Oh, God." That explained why the Forest Service had been so quick to send an investigator. The death of a federal employee in the line of duty gets an immediate investigation. Better the gentle Ortega than some pit bull of an FBI agent anyway. "Where?"

"Just outside the black."

"Why did he leave the black?"

"We don't know. We were wondering if you could tell us anything."

"Not much. The smoke was very dense. I lost sight of him. I became confused. I thought I was skiing."

"You were severely dehydrated. That can cause hallucinations."

"I called to Hogue, but he never answered. You couldn't tell where you were, whether you were going up or down, the smoke was so thick."

"That's how Ramona found you, you know. She said she heard you calling Hogue."

"She wrapped me in her fire shelter and told me I would be all right. I knew it was a woman, but I didn't know who. I was pretty out of it at that point."

"Did you hear anything else?"

"I thought I heard a voice before Ramona came, but that was all."

"You will let us know if you remember more?"

"Sure. What caused the fire?" There hadn't been a cloud in the sky, and I hadn't seen any lightning strikes, wet or dry.

"Our arson unit is investigating," Henry Ortega said. "The chief of the unit wants to talk to you." He handed me a card with the name Sheila S. A. McGraw on it. The phone number, I noticed, was in the Duke City and it had the same first three digits as mine.

"The office is in Albuquerque?"

"Yes. The Southwest Interagency Coordinating Center is on Gold Street. Will you call Sheila as soon as you get back to town?"

"Okay."

"Take care of yourself."

"Thanks," I said. This was the man, I thought, who should have counseled Ramona. He had the manner of a gentle priest, and a priest might be more acceptable to her than a counselor in a business suit. Black robes had been around the reservation for a long time. Ortega had been so kind that I suspected a bad cop was lurking outside the door and would come in next to attempt to browbeat a confession out of me, but nobody did. I didn't feel any guilt myself, but that didn't mean I had nothing to confess. Mike Marshall's blowup on the mountain wasn't something I wanted to discuss with the Forest Service yet.

The doctor came back, examined me again, told me I could leave in the morning and to quit smoking. That seemed easy enough now, but who knew how long the feeling would last.

I called the Kid at the shop and could hear his parrot, Mimo, squawking in the background. "Where are you?" he asked.

"In the hospital in Oro."

"*Híjole!* What happened?"

"I got caught in a forest fire on Thunder Mountain."

"Are you all right, Chiquita?"

"I'm okay," I said. "I'm going to be released tomorrow. Could you pick me up in the morning?"

"I can come now if you want."

"Tomorrow's okay."

"I'll leave after work tonight."

"Thanks, Kid."

"*De nada,*" he replied.

Later Eric Barker called. "We are so glad you weren't injured," he said.

"Me, too. Did you get out all right?" I asked him.

"Mike saw the flames on his way down the mountain. We drove out in his car and called the Forest Service."

"Ramona Franklin rescued me, you know."

"I heard," said Eric. "You'll call us when you get back to town?"

"Yes," I said.

* * *

There are several roads that will get you from Oro to Albuquerque. They're all scenic, they all take about the same amount of time. The northern route passes through the small towns of southern Colorado that rely on the resort trade for survival. It crosses the border into Chama and Tierra Amarilla, towns that rely on hunting and beauty for their survival. It's been said that the business of northern New Mexico is poverty, and the towns there are known to be suspicious of outsiders, even outsiders with Spanish surnames. But that could be changing. A latte bar, I'd heard, was opening in Chama. The Hispanic route passes through two national forests; much of it is high and green.

Another way passes through Indian country, which has its own allotment of poverty and beauty. The beauty here is in the big blue sky and the streaked red cliffs that reveal different levels of color and time, a white year, a red year, a year of rain, a year of fire. The Indian route goes through a number of the smaller reservations: Southern Ute, Jicarilla Apache, Jemez, Zia, Santa Ana. It misses the big one, the Navajo Nation, but it's still the road northern Navajos would take to get to Albuquerque. It's the road Ramona Franklin must have taken between her two lives. I owed her my life; I wanted to understand her better.

"Let's go home through Aztec and Cuba," I said to the Kid when he got to my hospital room.

He made a face, his second. The first had been when he saw how wasted I looked. "Why you want to do that?"

"It's pretty," I said.

He shrugged. "Any way you go is pretty."

"There's a good restaurant in Cuba. I'll take you to lunch."

"We can get there from Abiquiu."

"I want to go Route 44."

"I don't like that road." I knew why—nobody drove NM 44 unless he didn't know any better or had no choice—but the Kid told me anyway. *"Es el camino de la muerte,"* he said. The highway of death, one of New Mexico's infamous slaughter alleys. You couldn't blame it on the weather or on the curves. It rarely snowed or rained on Route 44. In many places the road was straight as an arrow. You could blame it on the bars at either end, the two lanes in between and the lack of a concrete wall median. Someone coming from one of the bars with a blood-alcohol level high enough to make a buffalo comatose fell asleep or passed out and plowed across the highway into the oncoming lane. And it was never just one person in the target vehicle. It was always a family, three or even four generations turned into roadkill by drink.

I looked at the clock on the wall: eight-thirty. "Nobody will be out yet."

"They'll be coming home after drinking all night," the Kid said.

"I'll drive if you want."

"It's my truck, Chiquita. You're sick."

"I'm not that sick."

"I drive. Just tell me why you want to do this." Maybe he thought I was under the irrational influence of sniffing smoke, but I had my reasons.

"Ramona Franklin grew up on the reservation near Farmington. She must drive 44 on her way back and forth to Albuquerque. I thought driving the road might help me understand her." It's my belief that you should never judge a woman until you've driven a mile in her vehicle on her roads. This wouldn't be Ramona's vehicle, but hers was also likely to be a truck. This was pickup country. "Do you remember what Gordon House said after the accident that killed the Cravens family?" The House case was one of New Mexico's most notorious traffic fatalities. On Christmas Eve three little girls and their mother were wiped out.

"What?" the Kid asked.

"That a trial wouldn't accomplish anything. That it should be settled the Navajo way. That he ought to get together with the family and talk it out."

"So?"

"That's what Ramona said to me. She wants to talk to the Barker family, but Nancy Barker won't talk to her. She saved my life; I'm wondering if rescuing me makes up in her mind for the loss of Joni Barker's life." That was the tip of the mountain, but there were layers upon layers underneath.

"Was Ramona to blame for Joni Barker's death?"

"Some people think she could have prevented it, some people think she couldn't. The question for me is what Ramona thinks."

It was getting too complex for the Kid. Easier to put the pedal to the metal and drive the road. "All right," he said. "*Vamos.*"

South of the Bloomfield oil fields I began coughing and didn't stop until we reached a trading post where I bought myself some cough drops. Route 44 is a great road for old trucks, and the Kid is a connoisseur. He pointed them out to me as he drove. "That's a '49 Chevy," he said. "That one's a '62 Ford."

"Sixty-two isn't *that* old," I said.

Trucks last forever in the dry New Mexico air and there's no inspection to ground you for a broken tailpipe or lack of turn signals. The older trucks have a rounded shape that's a pleasure to look at—adobe on wheels. It would be a pleasure to own one, too, if you didn't have to rely on it to take you one hundred miles to work or the store.

We went through a lot more empty space and passed a lot more old trucks before we reached Cuba. I hadn't been getting any adrenaline buzz from Route 44 or from wondering if any of those great old trucks had my name on them. Maybe I'd been adrenalined out. The Kid listened to Los Lobos and the Gipsy Kings, kept his mind on the road, and didn't talk much, leaving my mind free to think about Ramona Franklin. It must have been a big step for her to leave the reservation and move to Albuquerque, worrying, maybe, about whether the car would make it or not. It had to be a giant step to become the only Indian woman on a hotshot crew. The money was good. It would buy a reliable car, a comfortable place to live, toys and clothes for her daughter. How much did that mean to Ramona? Speculation was useless, but easy in the big empty. She had saved my life. But why mine? I had to ask. Why not Hogue's? If I was yelling for help, hadn't he been yelling, too? The even bigger question was what had caused the East Canyon fire that had endangered me and killed Hogue?

We stopped at Bruno's Restaurant in Cuba and sat in the courtyard under the ceiling of latillas so freshly cut that the leaves were still on. I had a sopapilla stuffed with meat and green chile. Nothing like a hit of green chile to clear your head.

The Kid bit into his burrito and the *chicharrones* crunched. "You learn anything about Ramona?" he asked.

"Lots of people can't wait to get away from the place they grow up. You did it, I did it. Right?" I hit the ground running when I departed Ithaca, New York. The Kid and his family had been forced out of Buenos Aires and into Mexico.

"Right," he said.

"Could you or would you want to go back?"

"In the beginning I did, but not anymore."

"Me neither." But we didn't come from the Navajo Nation with traditions that went back forever. "Ramona's job must mean a lot to her."

"It's a good job, no?"

"In some ways. It's also very dangerous."

"That's why the pay is good."

"Right."

"Some people like the danger. I'm hiring a new guy next week." Legal or illegal, I didn't ask. The Kid's business was expanding. He was making it in his new world.

"Good," I said.

* * *

We saw a lot more beauty before encountering the fast-food strip at Bernalillo and I enjoyed every bit of it. I could have turned into a white light or a black hole on Thunder Mountain, but I wouldn't have been seeing any red cliffs, tasting any green chile, listening to the Gipsy Kings, or resting my head on the Kid's shoulder if it hadn't been for Ramona. I called her the minute we got back to Albuquerque, but there was no answer.

9

The next day I slept until noon, snuggled up in my adobe home. Nothing like a mud hut to make you feel cool, calm, and sheltered. As I couldn't cough and sleep at the same time, sleeping gave my throat a chance to heal. The Kid had spent the night but gone off to work without waking me. Usually when he stays over, he just kind of shows up. But last night he'd planned far enough ahead to bring a change of clothes, and yesterday's blue jeans dangled from the bedpost.

He'd already called Anna to tell her what had happened on Thunder Mountain. I called her to find out what had happened in my office.

"Not much," Anna said. "How you doin'? You okay?"

"I'm all right."

"That Indian woman saved your life?"

"Yeah."

"You owe her."

I already knew that. I called Ramona again and got no answer. Then I called Sheila McGraw's office and made an appointment for the following day. After that I went back to sleep. Sometimes sleep is an elusive lover, but sometimes it's there when you need it. This was good sleep, deep sleep, sleep with the potential to heal. I didn't wake up again until the Kid arrived with Lotta Burgers and curly fries at six, and even then he had to shake me to rouse me.

"Who is Joe, Chiquita?" he asked. "You were talking about Joe in your sleep last night."

"I was?"

"Yes."

"I was doing that in the hospital, too, the nurses said. Joe's my father."

"I never hear you call him Joe."

"Usually I called him Dad, but he liked to be called Joe. That's how I remember him. When we were little he taught my brother and me to skate on the Irish Pond. Every winter he measured the ice to see if it was thick enough, and when it snowed he shoveled the snow off for us. When I wanted to play basketball he put up a net. He bought me my first pair of skis. He never skied himself, but he always encouraged me." My father, who worked for the phone company for thirty years, encouraged me to do all the things he couldn't or wouldn't do himself: to take risks, to finish college, to ski, to become a lawyer, and to never work for anyone else. After he died I completed his life. I graduated from college, became a skier, went to law school, and eventually started my own practice. I lived in Mexico for a while, which he would have loved to have done. I ended up in New Mexico, where he would also have enjoyed living. Joe and I were both sun seekers. After my brother joined the army, my father and I were left alone. The major relationships build their own kind of house. The one that Joe and I built was a snug and isolated cabin with a wood stove and no room for anyone else. The Kid and I shared twelve hundred square feet (when he stayed here, which had become more and more often), but the house our relationship inhabited had lots of rooms, lots of doors; some of them (the kitchen) were opened rarely, some of them (the empty room) were kept closed. "I was a good skier, Kid. I could ski better than most of the men on the hill. Do you believe that?"

"Why not? You have *mucho determinación* when you want to do something. Why don't you ski now?" You only had to look out the window to see that we had mountains year-round and in a few months they'd be covered with snow. "The cigarettes?"

"No. I smoked then. I don't know why I quit exactly. I was at my peak. After my father died I had a perfect day and I didn't want to ski anymore. That's when I decided to go to back to school. When I passed out in the fire I was reliving that day, and I saw my father at the base of the mountain calling to me."

"My father does that sometimes in my dreams," the Kid said. "He calls to me from the end of the soccer field."

"Are they asking us to join them or telling us not to?"

"Not to or we would be dead, no?"

"Maybe."

"When you learn a sport you never forget it. It stays with you your whole life."

"I don't know, Kid. Skiing isn't like riding a bicycle. I don't know if I could do it again. The equipment is different now. I'm not in great shape."

"I mean it stays in your attitude."

"You mean I have a skier's attitude?" These days that meant expensive skis and boots. I wasn't a person who'd chosen to earn or spend a lot of money, and I'd already been a ski bum.

"You have no fear, Chiquita," he said. "That's what I mean."

No fear or no sense. I had a feeling of twenty-year-old invincibility that lingered no matter what the pushing-forty evidence indicated. One thing I could say about my life was that I'd lived it. There'd be no one left to do that on my behalf. Was there anything wrong with still feeling like an invincible twenty-year-old? It had taken me into some dark places, some light places, some very interesting places. If you went into the past looking for hurt and abuse, you'd find them. If you went looking for accomplishment, you'd find a platform to spring from. You can master more than the mountain when you learn how to ski. That was what Joe had taught me.

Because my appointment with Sheila McGraw was for nine in the morning I approached the Forest Service's office on Gold from my home on Mirador instead of from my office on Lead. I drove down Edith past the new warehouses, the old pawnshops, and the bars with topless dancers. Albuquerque is a one-story town, a place where development doesn't climb, it crawls—although we do have a couple of skyscrapers downtown that can be seen from all over the city. They're the tallest buildings for miles, lightning rods in a storm. From the foothills in winter the downtown buildings are tombstones floating on a cloud of smog. From the West Mesa in any season they'll glow like rosy pink candles in the setting sun. There's an ongoing debate here about whether the sunset's afterglow is the color of watermelon or the color of blood. I call it watermelon-blood. The buildings of downtown are ugly in some lights, rose colored in others, but compared to most cities they're not imposing.

On the other hand, a fire the size of downtown is very imposing. I'd seen it and I'd seen it in motion. I'd heard it roar and hiss. It left me looking at downtown from a different perspective. I cut over to Third, stopped at the traffic light on Tijeras, and, while I waited for it to change, counted the stories in the Hyatt Regency. I'd reached twelve before the guy behind me leaned on his horn. "All right, all right," I said, and stepped on the gas.

I'd found a way to measure the fire. If anybody asked I could always say I'd been in a twelve-story blaze. That's something guys do, compare distance to a football field and height to the number of stories in a building. But when you get down to it, what other landmarks do we have? I do know that the more precise your figures and the more emphatically you present them, the less likely you are to be challenged.

85

I parked the Nissan and walked to 517 Gold, a government-issue gray building. Sheila S. A. McGraw wasn't a middle-aged guy looking around at the changes taking place in the Forest Service with regret and looking forward to retirement with longing. She was a woman who had to be older than she looked—around twenty-five. She was small with quick and nervous gestures, shiny black hair, and a complexion like the finish on an expensive tea cup. Her hair was cut short and straight. She wore glasses with dark rims that were too big for her face. They slid down her nose; she pushed them back up. She never lifted the glasses either to read or to look across the room. Maybe the prescription was weak or the glasses were an attempt to make her appear older and duller.

"That was quite an experience you had," she began.

"It was."

She looked down at a report on her desk. "Have you thought of anything you might have missed or forgotten to tell Henry Ortega?"

"No."

"Are you sure? He mentioned you were still groggy when you talked."

Maybe I was then, but I was clearheaded now. "I'm sure," I said.

"I'd like to go over a couple of points."

"Okay."

"Where were you when you first saw the smoke?"

"About halfway down the mountain."

"Any idea what time that was?"

"Some time after two. The first time we saw it, Hogue thought it was road dust and we kept on hiking."

She shook her head. "Bad mistake," she said.

"Very." It had cost Hogue his life. "About fifteen minutes later we saw the blowup. Then we began to run."

She straightened her glasses. "Your clients are Joni Barker's parents. Correct?"

"Right."

"Where were they that afternoon?"

"They waited for us in the parking lot. Nancy Barker was too upset to go back to the scene of the previous fire."

"I'll want to talk to them."

"We'll discuss it."

"Why didn't Mike Marshall come down the mountain with you and Hogue?"

"He was in a hurry. Haven't you talked to him yet?"

"Not yet. He's on my list."

I figured it was Mike or his lawyer's job to tell her what he'd said and done on the mountain, but if he didn't and that affected me or my clients, I'd have to do it for him. "Do you know what started the fire?"

"When we begin an arson investigation, first we exclude other causes such as lightning, accidents, or electrical. There were no reports of lightning. There are no electric lines in the area. There were no campfires burning that we know of. Someone might have been playing with matches, but we found a splatter pattern to the ignition points that indicates the fire was started by fusees. Someone ran through the drainage torching bushes, and it was done at a moment when winds would be gusting uphill."

"When I first saw the smoke there were no winds. It hovered over the drainage."

"That didn't last long, did it?"

"No. A few minutes later it was the size of a twelve-story building."

"Twelve stories?" She peered at me through the clear camouflage glasses.

"Something like that."

"We're calling this fire Thunder Mountain Two. It followed a similar pattern to Thunder Mountain One. It raced up the west side of the canyon, then jumped the drainage to the east. Once they get going, fires have a mind of their own, but there are a couple of things that are predictable about southwestern canyon fires. Piñon and juniper burn hot and fast. Winds pick up in the afternoon. There are updrafts in the daytime, downdrafts at night. Whoever started that fire either knew it was the optimum moment to torch the East Canyon or"—Sheila paused for effect—"was lucky. All firefighters carry fusees and they all know how to start fires. It's part of their job. The only person who knows how to start fires better than a firefighter is an arson investigator." She smiled. "There were several firefighters in the East Canyon that day. No arson investigators that I know of."

And more than one of the firefighters was carrying fusees. I'd seen them on Eric and I'd seen them on Mike. Ramona had been carrying a fire shelter and she was probably carrying the rest of the paraphernalia, too. "Fusees aren't that hard to come by, are they?" I asked.

"Not really. It's possible that some had been left behind on the mountain or at the encampment of the previous fire. We're still investigating the area and keeping it closed to the public."

"How long will that take?"

"We should be done by the end of the week."

"What happened to the house in the canyon?"

"It went up in smoke."

Her eyes were bright behind the clear lenses. "An interesting fact about Thunder Two is that whoever started it didn't go to much trouble to hide his—or her—actions. Another interesting fact is that there were people all over this mountain when it burned, and one of them died." Which made the crime more than arson. It made it manslaughter or murder in the third, second, or possibly even first depending on what premeditation there'd been.

"Has Hogue's autopsy been completed yet?"

"The fire killed him, we know that. But whether Hogue wandered into it, was pushed, or was incapacitated somehow and left to burn, we don't know. The body was badly burned. When a fire is that hot the muscles contract with such force that the bones are shattered. One motive for arson is crime concealment. People will set fires to destroy a body or hide what they did to it."

"Yeah, but burning down a mountain to incinerate a corpse is a little like torching a barn to destroy a mouse, isn't it?"

"That doesn't mean it isn't done. Does anybody in the business think crime is a rational act?"

Nobody that I knew.

Sheila looked at the report on her desk. "It says here Ramona Franklin was carrying a fire shelter and she wrapped it around you. Why you? I have to ask. Why not Hogue?"

"I haven't spoken to Ramona yet. I gather she heard me yelling and didn't hear him. It was very smoky in the black. Visibility was zero."

"Do you know Ramona well?" For me, one advantage to the thin lenses was that they didn't soften or distort her expression. She gave me the hard-eyed look of a falcon analyzing a piece of meat.

"No."

"I need to talk to Ramona and I haven't been able to locate her. If you hear from her, tell her to call me."

"Okay."

"Another common motive for arson, maybe even the most common motive, is revenge," she continued. "A guy's screwing around, the girlfriend gets pissed, sets his bed on fire. Or . . ." She paused with an actress's sense of dramatic timing. "Someone gets fired, torches the company store and/or the boss. In this case I consider the East Canyon the company store."

And the boss would be Tom Hogue.

"Is there any possibility you were the object of revenge?" she asked.

This investigation had put me in an interesting position. I was a witness, a victim, and possibly even a perp. Not only that, I represented two other possible perps and knew two more. But an object for revenge? From who? Brink? He'd left of his own volition, and besides, he was happier where he was. As for Anna, she'd rather comb her hair than play with matches. "I only have one employee and she was back at the office," I said.

"How about ex-lovers? Jealous wives?"

"Nah." I'd been clean on that score for a long time. "Besides, I wasn't supposed to be there. The original plan had been for the helicopter to pick me up."

"Why'd you change that plan?"

"Hogue wanted to walk out. I decided to go with him."

"Did he radio the helicopter?"

"Yes."

"People with radios were all over that mountain. Any one of them could have picked up that conversation."

"What are the other motives?" I asked.

"There are people who like to play with fire and watch it burn. Thunder One was close to town; a lot of people saw it. One of them might have been a latent pyro who liked what he saw so much he wanted to watch another canyon go up in smoke. A fire can be pretty thrilling to watch. Then there's arson for profit. That was a large and expensive house that burned in the fire. Maybe the arsonist wanted the insurance money more than the house. There's civil disorder. A judge in Arizona just closed forests all over the Southwest to logging to protect the habitat of the endangered spotted owl. Someone—a logger, a spotted owl lover or hater—could have been protesting Forest Service policy. There are people out there who don't believe in the Forest Service's policy of fire suppression, who believe we should just let forests and adjacent houses burn. Firefighters have been known to start fires to get work. When that happens near an Indian reservation they call it a powwow fire. And don't forget arson by stupidity. Arsonists aren't the brightest people in the world. We had one of those recently right here in town."

"Melloy Dodge?"

"Right. That place was an OSHA nightmare. The paints were stored in a room with no ventilation where guys were playing with firecrackers." She shook her head. Her glasses slid down her nose and she pushed them back up. "You'll set up the appointment with your clients?"

"I'll talk to them." That was as far as I was willing to go. It seemed to me that the interview was over and I was getting ready to leave, but Sheila wasn't done yet.

"I have a question for you," she said.

"Shoot."

"How'd you get a guy's name?"

"From my uncle who was with the Tenth Mountain Division in World War II. He died near Cortina, Italy."

"Do people ask you about it a lot?"

"All the time."

"I had an unusual name myself. I got tired of explaining it, so I changed it."

"What was it?"

"Singing Arrow."

That's what the S.A. stood for. There was one advantage to being a postwar baby, you got a war hero's name. It could be a burden, but it wasn't a joke. "Your parents named you Singing Arrow McGraw?"

"Do you believe it? They were hippies." The hippie gene

seems to skip a generation. When the parents are hippies, the kids are yuppies, but the grandchildren might turn out to be hippies all over again. There was nothing hippie about Sheila. Although she did have an offroad sense of humor, she was all brains and business. There was a time when intelligence in a woman was a fierce dog on a short leash constantly held in check, but Sheila McGraw's intelligence seemed more like a semi-trained falcon, a kestrel that kept escaping from her, flying off and doing rollovers or zeroing in on something it wanted to inspect.

"How'd you get into arson investigation?" I asked her.

"I was a chemistry major. I wanted some security in my life. I was planning to go to med school, but this job came along. I liked it and I stayed."

I had one more question: How old are you, Sheila McGraw? But I knew better than to ask.

10

On my way back to Hamel & Harrison I stopped and bought some Ricola throat lozenges. There was a hole in my life I was hoping herbs and menthol would fill.

"You don't look too good," Anna greeted me when I entered the office.

"Pleasure to see you, too, Anna."

"You look like you've been through . . . "

"Hell?" I'd been in a fire, which is as close as you can come to the hell most of us know.

"Kind of tired."

"I'm tired of coughing. I'm tired of feeling like I'm full of smoke."

"You gonna quit?" she asked.

"Quit what?"

"Smoking."

"Maybe," I said. The desire was gone, but who knew how long it would stay that way. At least as long as I was full of smoke. There were people who'd light their last cigarette in an oxygen tent. There was still a possibility I wouldn't be one. I went into my office, popped a Ricola, and wondered who I ought to call first: Eric or Nancy Barker. Nancy, I decided; she was the one who'd made the initial contact. She wasn't home, so I tried Eric at UNM.

"Neil," he said, "when did you get back?"

"Saturday. I was at the arson investigator's office this morning," I said. "She wants to talk to you and Nancy. I think we ought to get together and discuss it. I tried Nancy, but she wasn't home."

"She was in town this morning. She'll be back after lunch. When would you like to get together?"

"The sooner the better."

"I have some free time this afternoon."

"How about one o'clock?"

"See you then," he said.

It's easier to evaluate people when you meet them on their own turf, one reason clients prefer to have their initial meeting with a lawyer in the lawyer's office. I would have preferred to have met Eric in his house or his classroom, or even a piñon-juniper forest, but I couldn't think of any way to set it up. When he showed up in his cotton shirt and khakis looking like an unmade bed, I realized it wouldn't have mattered where I'd met Eric Barker. He'd be the same wherever he was.

"How are you feeling?" he asked me.

"Not great. I keep coughing up black stuff."

"It takes awhile to get it out of your system." I'd

become one of a select group, I realized—those who'd survived fire. It was a bond he'd shared with Joni and now with me.

"A forest fire's a pretty terrifying experience," he said.

"It is."

"Everybody's afraid on a fire, all the time."

"What I was feeling went beyond fear. It was another dimension."

"You must have been dehydrated. That can cause hallucinations."

"Did that ever happen to you?"

"I never actually hallucinated on a fire, but I have gotten kind of dingy. I thought I could talk to the animals and the trees."

"Did they answer?"

"Sometimes." His smile was quick and slight, but it was a pleasure to see.

"My experience was more like a dream than an hallucination," I said. "I was skiing in New England. It was a perfect day, the best day I ever had skiing."

"I taught Joni to ski," Eric said.

"Mike showed me a video. She was fantastic."

"I raised her to be a skier and a firefighter." A light came on in his eyes when he talked about Joni. It was a light I'd seen in my own father's eyes. It was unprofessional to be looking into Eric Barker's eyes, I knew, but I was drawn to the light. He was a teacher, however, who'd worked for years with younger women. He knew when too deep went too far, when too personal was unprofessional. He straightened up and changed the subject.

"What did the investigator have to say?" he asked.

"That the fire was caused by arson."

"That doesn't surprise me."

"She wants to talk to you and Nancy as witnesses." And maybe even as perps, but I didn't get into that yet.

"I don't have a problem with that." He was staring at his hands, looking at traces of the fires he'd been on, maybe, seeing memories in the ashes. "What do you think?"

I gave him a lawyer's answer. "It would be better not to. Talking to investigators can be a risky business."

"I'll discuss it with Nancy," he replied.

"What did you and Nancy do while you waited?" I asked.

"I took a walk."

"How long were you gone?"

"An hour."

"Did you take your pack?"

"Yes."

"What did Nancy do while you were gone?"

"Sat under the tree."

"Did you see or hear anything suspicious on your walk?"

"No. Nothing. It was very quiet. Around three I began to smell smoke."

"When did Mike get back?"

"Three-fifteen."

"Did he seem angry or upset?"

"He was agitated. He'd seen the fire."

"Was he concerned about Ramona?"

"He didn't mention it."

I'd been circling, but it was time to get to the point. "Sheila McGraw, the chief investigator, believes the fire was started by a professional."

Eric shrugged. "Firefighters are trained to start backfires, but it doesn't take that much skill to start a forest fire."

"She said there was a splatter pattern to the ignition points that indicated the fire was started by fusees and that it was set at a time when the blaze would have maximum effect."

Eric's eyes headed for my open window.

"What do you think could have been the arsonist's motive? To kill me? To kill Hogue? To make a statement about Forest Service policy?"

"Why would anybody would want to kill you?" he asked.

"I don't know."

"There could well have been people with a grudge against Hogue. He's their P.R. man and a symbol of the Forest Service just as much as Smokey the Bear is. Someone might have borne a grudge against the whole department and taken it out on him. On the other hand, people will light fires just to watch them burn. The fact that you and Hogue and Mike and Ramona were on the mountain may have had nothing to do with it. The arsonist might have not even known you were on the mountain. We heard the helicopter and we thought the pilot had come back to pick you up. Wasn't that the plan?"

"Yeah, but that plan changed. Hogue decided to walk out and I went with him," I said. "Did you see Ramona anywhere on the mountain that day?"

"No."

"Apparently she tied a wet bandanna over my nose and mouth, wrapped me in her fire shelter, and split. I was barely conscious at the time. I knew someone was helping me, but I didn't know who. Henry Ortega, the arson investigator, told me it was Ramona."

"Firefighters have been using wet bandannas since 1910. You'd think there'd be some new technology by now, wouldn't you?"

"You'd think so. Ramona told Henry Ortega she rescued me because she heard me calling for help. She said she didn't hear Hogue."

"Firefighters only carry one shelter," Eric said, which meant she could only save one person. "Have you talked to her yet?"

"No. She's not answering her phone. Do you think that to a Navajo saving one person's life would in any way compensate for causing another person's death?"

"You were at the fire scene. Do you think she was the cause of anyone's death?"

"The South Canyon looked like bare skin with razor burn and trees for stubble the day I was there. It was hard to tell what Ramona could or couldn't have seen when the canyon was full of brush and trees. Hogue and I didn't see the fire until we were right on top of it."

"Sometimes bad things just happen, Neil. Sometimes conditions are so severe there's nothing anyone can do."

Those were the words that got him through the day, but if I believed them I'd have to take down my license to practice law. "Whether Ramona saw the fire or she didn't, the government should have provided aerial surveillance," I said. "The government should have done a lot of things to protect the firefighters that it didn't do."

"Are we talking negligence suit?" Eric asked. There was still hope in the gray eyes, but that was a fire I was about to put out.

"I think there's cause for action." And I wasn't seeing dollar signs when I said it either. "I don't have to prove guilt beyond a reasonable doubt. We only need a preponderance of evidence in a civil suit."

"Damn," Eric said softly. He stared out the window. "You know what I'd like to do right now?"

"Talk it over with Nancy?"

"No. I'd like to go down to Baja, get in a boat, and drift out to sea."

"Do it," I said.

"I might never come back."

"You'll come back."

"How do you know?"

"Because you didn't raise your daughter to run away from trouble," I said.

11

It was a quarter to two by Anna's clock when Eric left. If I got in my car and drove over the mountain I could be at Nancy's house in Cedar Crest in an hour. I was having trouble getting back in the office groove anyway. I could have called Nancy and told her I was coming, but I didn't. Eric had already said she'd be home.

"I'm kind of tired. I think I'll take the rest of the afternoon off," I told Anna.

"You'll be in tomorrow?"

"Yeah," I said.

I went the back way to Cedar Crest, through the village of Placitas, up the winding dirt road, past the cave where Placitas Man was found and later discovered to be a hoax. I continued through the woods and over the mountain. "Closed for the Winter" the sign said where the pavement ended; it always said that—even now in August. There were quaking aspens at the higher elevations and they were already turning yellow. About halfway up I stopped at Las Huertas picnic area, parked the Nissan, and walked to the stream that flows through the canyon. I sat on a rock wall and listened to the water rush under a downed log and over a rock. There's enough Easterner left in me that every now and then I get a craving for water. It has a way of smoothing rough edges, but after a few minutes of soothing I began to hear crying in the gurgling. New Mexico's streams, rivers, and ditches are haunted by the spirit of La Llorona, the woman who drowned her children and wanders our waterways weeping. The wide-open spaces were looking good again. I got in the Nissan and drove to the ridge top where the view stretches nearly to Texas.

The road on the east side of the Sandias is paved; it's the road the skiers, tourists, and hikers use. The weather is cooler and wetter over here, and the forest is lush. If this side of the mountain had ever been timbered, it was a long time ago. Second-growth forests tend to be monochromatic and boring. This forest had shades and levels of green from deep ponderosa to silvery blue spruce interspersed with crooked white aspen.

The Barkers lived at the base of the mountain on Aspencade Drive in Cedar Crest. My map showed Aspencade to be parallel straight lines ending in parallel dotted lines, a gravel road turning to dirt. Sometimes it's hard to tell where the gravel leaves off and the dirt begins. The bumps on Aspencade were spaced at intervals that made the Nissan rattle like a bucket of bolts whenever I exceeded fifteen miles an hour. In Santa Fe there's a cachet to living on dirt roads, but they drive Mercedes-Benz jeeps up there and don't have to get up every morning and go to work. That's one reason I don't live in the East Mountains; it's too big a mind change to drive from rural to urban and back every day. It's simpler to live and work in the same zone.

The Barkers' house was at the edge of the forest, where sunbeams were slipping through the branches of the pines and landing on the pine-needle floor. It was easy to see how a kid growing up here would want to protect trees. The house was wood frame with lots of east-facing windows, a pitched roof, and a large deck. A Saturn was parked at one end of the driveway. At the other was a vegetable garden with corn, tomatoes, and squash. As I got out of my car I was greeted by a squirrel screeching and dropping a pinecone to the deck. Nancy came to the door. "Neil," she called, "what are you doing here? Come on up."

Climbing the stairs to the deck brought on another coughing fit. "You all right?" Nancy asked with a motherly concern in her voice.

"Yeah."

"What brings you over here?" She was very surprised to see me, and as insistent on making that point as the squirrel was on making his. Her mouth was a slash of red lipstick. Her hair was a blond helmet. She wore khaki hiking shorts, sandals that gripped her big toe, and a T-shirt. The green ribbon was pinned across her heart. It takes discipline for a grieving woman to put on lipstick and get dressed every morning. Another mother I'd known who'd lost her daughter had never gotten out of her bathrobe again.

"I was taking the back road to Santa Fe; I get tired of I-25. I'd thought I'd stop by to see how you were doing," I answered, proving, if only to myself, that I could lie as well as I could cough.

"More important, how are you doing?"

"I'm okay."

"Come on in and have some tea with honey. That'll help your cough." I followed her into the house, which was done in a style I'd call Appalachian cabin. The furniture was made out of logs and there were quilted fabrics on the walls, the pillows, and the windows. An unfinished quilt with a red pattern on a white background lay on the sofa. Nancy must have been working on it when I showed up. The house was cozy and neat, no fuzzy film on the coffee table, no telltale dust balls under the sofa. No TV that I could see. Nancy put the water on and began banging mugs around the kitchen. "What would you like?" she called. "I have Constant Comment, Grandma's Tummy Mint, Emperor's Choice, Red Zinger."

"Red Zinger," I said.

She came back with a steaming ceramic mug and a jar of honey on a tray. I stirred in the honey with a plastic beehive on a stick and put the mug down on the end table. Nancy lifted the mug and placed a coaster underneath. She pushed the quilt aside and sat beside me on the sofa.

"You're making a quilt?" I asked.

"It'll give me something to do until school starts. I have to keep busy or I'll go crazy." It's hard enough to stay occupied alone in a house in the woods without a death to deal with. With a tragedy it would have been all too easy to pull the curtains, turn on the TV, smoke Marlboros, drink tequila, and enter the dark place looking for light. Nancy picked up a needle and threaded it. Her relentless determination made me wonder if she wasn't taking mother's latest little helper—Prozac. It's the perfect substance to keep a woman working and smiling from dawn to dusk.

"You've been on the mountain now. What do you think? Do we have a case?" Nancy asked me.

"Mike gave a convincing demonstration that dropping the packs wouldn't have saved anyone's life. It was a very steep and dangerous place to attempt to fight a fire. There should have been aerial surveillance. I can understand how hard it would have been for Ramona to see the fire. There should have been better training. There should have been better weather forecasting. The fact that that information wasn't passed on to the firefighters is gross negligence in my mind."

Nancy's eyes had the red fire of a deer trapped in the headlights or a woman caught off guard by the camera, a woman who was far too angry to be on Prozac. She appeared to be getting by substance-free. "They never should have sent the crew in there just to save somebody's trophy home. Never!" she said jabbing the quilt with her needle.

She lived so close to the woods herself I had to wonder what she'd have done if her house had been threatened.

"It makes me so goddamn angry. Did you see how big that house was?"

"It's gone now," I said.

"Good."

"Do you blame Hogue for the South Canyon?"

"I blame everybody in the Forest Service. I'm mad at them for sending Joni to Thunder Mountain. I'm mad at them for not giving the firefighters any support. I'm mad at Ramona for living. I'm mad at Joni for dying. Dumb, I know, but I can't help it."

Emotions can be like fire. Sometimes they are easily ignited, sometimes not, but once they get burning it's in their nature to get out of control. "Does the fact that Hogue died up there make any difference to you in terms of pursuing the lawsuit?"

"No. He was just a symbol. I want to get the people who made the decisions that killed my daughter."

"I talked to Eric earlier," I said.

"Oh? He didn't mention it."

"It was only about an hour ago. I tried to call you first but you weren't home. The arson investigator has determined that the East Canyon fire was caused by arson."

"That figures. I mean, what else could it have been?"

"They want to talk to you as part of the investigation."

"You're our lawyer. Do you have any objection to that?"

"It's always better not to talk to investigators. Did you see or hear anything while you waited? Anybody driving or walking up the road?"

"Not really," Nancy replied. "I think some vehicles went by, but I couldn't see them from where I sat."

"Under the cottonwood?"

"Right."

"When did Mike get back?"

"Around three."

"What kind of frame of mind was he in?"

"He was very upset. He'd seen the fire. We'd smelled the smoke. As soon as Mike returned we got into his car, drove out, and called the Forest Service. That fire was terrifying to watch. It would have been even more terrifying if we'd known you were on the mountain."

"Where did you think I had gone?"

"We heard the helicopter; we thought you must have left on it. We're very glad you survived, Neil." She looked up from her sewing. The red light was gone. Her eyes were a warm, concerned brown.

"Thanks," I said. "Did you see Ramona anywhere?"

"I never saw Ramona that day."

"Eric told me you waited alone in the parking lot for an hour while he took a walk in the woods."

She put down her sewing. "Eric told you he took a walk?"

"Didn't he?"

"Well, yeah, he did, but so did I. Didn't he tell you that?" The red light in her eyes was coming back.

"No."

"He must have forgotten."

"How long were you gone?"

"Forty-five minutes." She was very precise, but she wore no watch on her sewing wrist, I noticed, or on her other wrist.

"Who had the pack?"

"He left it with me."

"He told me he took it."

"He's wrong. I had it."

When Eric said he'd taken a walk, he'd given himself the window of opportunity to have started the fire. Now Nancy had done the same for herself. He might have been giving her an alibi when he'd told me he took the pack and she waited under the tree. She couldn't very well provide him with one; he'd already said he'd taken the walk. But when it comes to married couples the effect of both giving the other opportunity was the equivalent of both providing the other with alibis—a smoke screen. While a prosecutor and jury would expect a married couple to alibi each other, they wouldn't necessarily believe them. To give themselves and the other opportunity was more unexpected and, in a way, more believable. The federal government doesn't have spousal privilege. A spouse can be forced to testify against a spouse in a federal case, but when a husband and wife are your only witnesses and they have provided each other with the opportunity to commit the crime, it makes it very hard to convict either one of them. Who are you going to believe? When both people are respectable citizens, a conviction could be damn near impossible. From a defense lawyer's point of view divide and confuse can be good strategy, but it could make it impossible to represent both parties.

"Did you see or hear anything unusual while you walked?" I asked Nancy.

"Only the birds and the squirrels. What did Eric say about talking to the investigators?"

"He said he would discuss it with you."

"We'll want to cooperate. Could you set up the interview?"

"If that's what you want me to do. Would you prefer to be interviewed separately or together?"

She tied a knot, broke off a thread, stuck the needle in its cushion. "Together," she said.

I stood up to leave. "I'll be in touch."

She rose and shook the quilt loose to study her work. The red fabric on the white background had the zigzag pattern of snakes and lightning.

I retraced my route slowly down the gravel/dirt road, turned right on 14, got on I-40 West, and drove through Tijeras Canyon, where the road can be icy in winter and the wind treacherous at any time. It's another well-known *camino de la muerte*. My thoughts turned to life, death, murder, arson. With murder there's a definite object whether the killer knows the victim or not, but who knows where arson will lead? The motives have to be more complex.

I moved into the slow lane; a rig that hadn't seen traffic since Amarillo was hauling ass and breathing down my neck. The driver could have been popping ephedrine until he or she was bouncing off the walls. The driver wasn't trying to kill me per se, just anyone who got in the way.

12

I got off I-40 at Carlisle and drove to Mike Marshall's house. His red Subaru was parked in the driveway. The TV flickered through the blinds. I rang the bell, watched the TV go off, and waited for Mike to come to the door. Maybe he'd been reliving afternoons skiing with Joni, maybe he'd been watching baseball, maybe he'd been watching Oprah. It was late afternoon, Oprah hour in the Land of Enchantment. In my experience grief doesn't have a steady flow, it comes in waves. There are times of day when the waves wash in and others when they wash back out. Some people react to the inflow by hiding under their pillow, some get angry, some get drunk, some get angry and drunk—the most dangerous combination and one I hadn't come across on this case, not yet anyway. I prefer the total immersion route myself—on the principle that the fastest way out of pain is through it—but to follow that path you need experience or faith, something to make you believe you'll find light on the other side. Mike, I figured, didn't have the experience or the faith. The best path for him would be action, and that seemed to be the one he was taking. He opened the door wearing shorts and a T-shirt. He was drenched in sweat, his curls plastered to his forehead.

"Whew," he said, rubbing the sweat out of his eyes. "I've been working out."

"That's good, isn't it?"

"It helps. Come on in."

I followed him into the living room, where an exercise machine sprawled across the carpet like a giant bug. There wasn't much light, but enough to see the weights on the floor, a pile of laundry on the futon, dirty dishes on the dining room table. This was what the house looked like when he didn't know someone was coming.

He pulled a sweat suit off the pile on the sofa and yanked it over his T-shirt and shorts. He was bending over to tie his running shoes and I couldn't see his expression when he said, "I'm sorry. I've been meaning to call you. There are times when I just can't talk about it and this week has been one of them." He finished tying his shoes and looked up. "I need to get out of here. You want to get something to drink?"

It was all right with me, there was no place to sit in here. "Okay."

"How 'bout a lemonade or a soda?"

"Why not?"

"Let's go to the Juice Bar. It's right around the corner; we can walk. It'll give me a chance to cool off."

To me the walk felt more like a speed-up than a cooldown. Mike's pace was too fast for conversation; I had to struggle just to keep up. It gave me a chance to start coughing and him a chance to collect his thoughts. The Juice Bar had round tables and the metal chairs you find in an ice-cream parlor. I sat down in the first one available. Mike went to get me a glass of water.

"You sound like a firefighter," he said, giving that word all due respect.

I swallowed my water and asked for a lemonade. Mike ordered a Coke. "I feel like a firefighter," I said. "I feel like I'll be coughing up smoke until January."

"It'll go away eventually. I would have come back for you, you know, if I'd known you were still up there. Why did you hike out?"

"Because Hogue didn't think I was capable of it."

"That's the kind of guy he was."

"You didn't hear him talking on the radio?"

"No. I didn't use my radio that day. I had no reason to. That fire blew up really fast. Canyon fires do that. When we realized we couldn't do any good there, the Barkers and I drove out and notified the Forest Service." His Coke had arrived. He started sipping on the straw, slurping his way through the drink.

"The Barkers were both there when you reached the campground?"

"That's right."

"What kind of frame of mind were they in?"

He gave me a curious look. The Barkers were my clients; I was the one who was supposed to know their frame of mind if anyone did. But he answered the question. "Upset," he said. "They'd smelled the smoke. They were relieved to see me."

"Where was Ramona? Did you ever see her again that day?"

"I didn't see her after she left in the morning to leave her tribute," he said. He made his way rapidly through the Coke and the ice until he was sucking on air. He flagged down the waitress and ordered another.

"Your paths never crossed on the mountain?"

"Never. I understand a couple of firefighters found Ramona in the South Canyon and brought her out after the fire."

"That's what I heard. You haven't talked to her yourself?"

"No," he said, and he looked me right in the eye when he said it. His eyes seemed duller than they had before, as if a thirst had been quenched, a passion burned out or a point proven. "I haven't talked to her since she left that morning. I can't find her. She must have gone back to the Rez. You're very lucky she was there. She saved your life. Ramona can hang. She knows what to do around fire."

"Why did she save me? Why not Hogue?"

"That's something you'll have to ask Ramona."

"I can't find her, either. I've been calling and calling but there's no answer. You don't have her address, do you?"

"She lives in the South Valley. Two hundred Sunset Court. Turn west off of Isleta. It's near the end of the block."

"Thanks," I said. "Have you talked to Sheila McGraw yet?"

"Oh, yeah, she called me. I'm a prime arson suspect, aren't I? I've been mouthing off about the Forest Service. I was on the mountain. I was carrying fusees on my pack. I know how to use them."

"She does believe it was a professional job."

"I made an appointment to see her."

"Are you taking your lawyer?"

"What do I need a lawyer for? I'm telling the truth."

"Sheila wants to talk to Ramona, too. From her point of view we're all suspects: you, me, the Barkers, Ramona. The means and opportunity were available to all of us, separately or together." Although motive was a lot trickier.

"Hasn't the Forest Service caused the Barkers enough pain?"

"They've established that the fire was started by fusees. You carried them. Eric carried them. Since Ramona had a fire shelter, they're going to assume she was carrying a fully loaded pack and that she had them, too."

Mike looked into his glass and rattled the ice with the straw. "So she was carrying a pack. What was the motive? Ramona has a strong attachment to trees. She sees her job as saving them, not killing them."

"Revenge. The Forest Service was responsible for the death of someone you both loved. Hogue did threaten to fire you both."

"You didn't tell McGraw that, did you?"

"No," I admitted. "She didn't ask me what transpired

on the mountain. I didn't see it as my role to volunteer."

It's seldom a lawyer's role to volunteer.

"Really?" Mike asked.

"Really."

"Hogue couldn't fire me anyway; I'd already quit. If Ramona was worried about her job, the smart thing would have been to save Hogue's life, wouldn't it? Even the worst woman-hating racist wouldn't fire the Indian woman who'd saved his life."

"Maybe she couldn't find Hogue. The smoke was very thick." Or maybe she did find him. No one knew if he died before or during the fire. "Did you see anybody else on the mountain or any other vehicles on the road that day?"

"No, but you know how thick the brush and trees were. There could have been people all over the mountain that I didn't see. There are plenty of people around with a gripe against the Forest Service."

"Did you tell anybody else that you were meeting Hogue on Thunder Mountain?"

"No, but anybody could have seen and heard the helicopter flying in and known the Forest Service was around. A house went up in smoke, didn't it?"

"Yeah."

"Anyone looking for motive ought to be talking to the owner." He put his glass down on the table. "I proved my point about Joni, didn't I?"

"You proved to me that she wouldn't have survived the fire even if she had dropped her pack, if that's what you mean."

"Joni was a first-class firefighter. It pissed me off that she wasn't getting any recognition for that. So what if she didn't always go by the book? The best firefighters don't. How are you going to advise the Barkers about the suit?"

"I told them that I think there's cause for action. The government was negligent in a lot of areas. But whether the Barkers will choose to go ahead, I don't know. What do you think?"

"For myself I don't care anymore. I proved what I wanted to prove. But if it would make the Barkers feel better, I say go for it." He stood up; in his mind the conversation was over. "I need to get back to my workout. You can believe it or not, Neil, but I'm glad you survived."

"I believe it," I said.

I called Ramona when I got home. Still no answer.

The Kid came for dinner with a bag of burritos from Casa de Benevides under his arm. We washed them down— Tecate for him, tequila for me—watched TV for a while, and went to bed early. When I woke up in the morning he'd already left for work. I was getting used to seeing his clothes draped over the bedposts at the foot of the bed, but a new pile had gathered on the chair. That's the way it is when you own a house, a man starts moving in. There was still plenty of mess in my house, but that was my mess. This wasn't. I gathered up all the clothes as if I was headed for the laundry, but they weren't all dirty and I didn't feel like washing them even if they were. I took the pile into the empty room and opened the closet, empty except for the fire shelter. That was empty enough for me. The garage was not a viable alternative. The hall closet was stuffed full. I went back to my bedroom, opened my closet, hung up what went on hangers, and found a bureau drawer for the rest.

13

In the morning I talked to Sheila McGraw and set up the appointment with the Barkers for four the following afternoon. I called Nancy and Eric separately and asked them to meet me in my office together at three. They sat down in the chairs across from my desk. I got Eric his coffee with sugar and Nancy her water.

"You've given me different versions of the events at Thunder Mountain," I began. "Eric, you told me you took a walk with the backpack. Nancy, you said you both took walks but that you had the pack. This is a criminal investigation. I need to know what really happened. I can't represent both of you if you are divided." If I could only represent one, which one could be a tough choice. But I didn't really expect them to go their separate ways. They'd been married a long time. I figured they'd find a way to present a united front.

Eric looked at his wife. Nancy looked back. "We both took walks," she said.

"Together?"

"Separately," Nancy said.

"Then why did you tell me that only you did?" I asked Eric.

He watched the sugar dissolve in his coffee. "I forgot to mention it. It didn't seem important."

"I didn't go anywhere," Nancy said. "I just wandered around the trails."

"With the pack on your back?"

"Yes. I thought I might want some water. The water was in the pack."

Who was covering for whom? I wondered. Nancy had the rage to start a fire; Eric had the skill. If I'd been an investigative reporter I wouldn't have dropped it there, I'd have badgered and hounded them. But I wasn't a journalist, I was a lawyer. The fact that they had changed their stories didn't necessarily mean they were guilty of anything. They might have been protecting each other from the appearance of guilt before. They might be telling the truth now. When it came to the Barkers, my job was not to believe or disbelieve. Aside from the question of defending someone who might have put my life in danger, my job was to give both of them the best possible representation. If I couldn't accept those terms, I shouldn't accept the job. In spite of all that had gone up in smoke I could smell government negligence. I wouldn't want to think it was money that was driving me; I preferred to think it was the government's carelessness, its stupidity, and its shabby treatment of Joni and the Duke City Hotshots.

"Unless Sheila McGraw finds an arsonist who's willing to confess, this case could well go to trial. The Forest Service isn't going to let one of their own get killed without trying somebody for the crime. Whatever you say to Sheila today you could be asked to repeat in court."

"We understand," said Nancy.

"All right," said Eric, sipping at his sweetened coffee.

"You have nothing to add to what you've already told me?" Or subtract? I wondered.

"No," said Nancy.

"Nothing," said Eric.

"You'll be questioned as witnesses but also as potential suspects; you were on the mountain, you had the means, you had the opportunity, you were angry and upset. You don't have to answer her questions if you choose not to."

"We want to cooperate," said Nancy. "We want the government to find out who did this."

"Okay," I said, "let's get it over with."

On the way to Sheila's office I remembered I'd left the package with the photos and boots under my desk.

Sheila and Henry Ortega interviewed Nancy and Eric separately, as I'd suspected they would. Everyone played their roles to perfection, including me, but I had very little to do. Henry Ortega was the good cop—kind, gentle, concerned, not as well educated as Sheila, but people smart. He deferred to Sheila's rank, but he retained his dignity. He played the part of the soulful saxophone. Sheila was a snare drum drilling the Barkers with questions. She was quick, aggressive, skeptical. Nancy and Eric were concerned and cooperative citizens who stuck to their story. They had taken walks separately. Nancy had the pack. They were both back at the cottonwood when Mike came down the mountain at three-fifteen, breathless and agitated. They had smelled smoke, but didn't know the forest was on fire until Mike told them. They hadn't seen Ramona or anyone else on the mountain. Nancy might have heard a vehicle, but she didn't see one. They drove out with Mike in the Subaru and called the Forest Service. The only difference worth noting between them was that Eric wore a watch and Nancy didn't, but I might have been the only one who noticed that.

At the end of the interviews Henry Ortega asked both Barkers how they were coping with Joni's death. "As best we can," said Eric. "I keep busy," Nancy said. Did either of them know Tom Hogue? Eric had met Hogue before the trip to Thunder Mountain. Nancy hadn't. What did Eric think of him? "He did his job," Eric answered. "You must be very glad that your lawyer survived the fire," Henry said. "Oh, we are," they replied. Henry thanked the Barkers and the interviews were over.

Eric was last, and after his interrogation we were expecting Nancy to be waiting for us on a bench in the hallway, the same place Eric had waited for her. She wasn't there. Eric went looking for her while I went to the bathroom. When I came out Eric was gone, too. I figured they'd be waiting outside in the sunshine.

Sheila was standing in the doorway to the interrogation room when I came back down the hallway. "Neil, could you come in here for a minute. I want to talk to you," she said in a voice that reminded me of a principal about to scold me for smoking during recess. "That's 'a-l' as in 'pal,'" I remembered a grade-school principal saying, but even then I knew better than to believe it. The Forest Service hallway was dingy and institutional enough to remind me of the places where I went to school. Those hallways were where the tawdry high school dramas got played out.

"No, ma'am, I haven't been smoking," I felt like saying, "but your voice is making me crave a butt more than I have all week." I unwrapped a Ricola and popped it to help satisfy the urge. The Barkers' combined version of events was, I thought, as smooth and impervious as stone. Could Sheila possibly have known that very recently there'd been two different versions? I wondered. How smart was she anyway?

"Your clients were very cooperative," she said.

"Of course," I replied.

"You are aware that they provided each other with the window of opportunity, and the federal government doesn't recognize spousal privilege?"

I sucked on my Ricola, smothered a cough, and said not a word.

But it wasn't the Barkers Sheila wanted to talk about, it was Ramona Franklin, who had better means, motive, and opportunity than either of the Barkers and who hadn't made herself available for interrogation. "I'm still looking for Ramona Franklin. Do you have any idea where she is?" Sheila's eyes zeroed in on me through the glasses. You're going too far with this school-marm business, I thought.

"I am not Ramona's lawyer."

"She did save your life. I thought you two might have been in touch."

"We haven't."

"We tracked down her mother, who said Ramona brought her daughter to the mother's house on the reservation and that Mike Marshall picked her up there early on Friday and took her to Thunder Mountain. She said Ramona called the trading post and left a message that she'd be back for the daughter in a few days. Mrs. Franklin assumed Ramona had called from Albuquerque."

"As I said, I don't know where she is."

"If you do hear from Ramona tell her that it will be better for her if I don't have to send out the posse."

"I'll do that," I said. "How's the on-site investigation going?"

"Pretty good. We're just about to finish up."

"When do you plan to reopen the area?"

"Sunday. Thanks for your help."

"*De nada,*" I said.

When schoolgirls want to get out from under authority's thumb they go outside and smoke a cigarette. There's usually somebody there to hang out and be naughty with. Nowadays all smokers seem delinquent, and you can almost count on the cloud of smoke that hovers outside every office building, the butts littering the sidewalk, the smokers leaning up against the wall chatting and enjoying every puff. The sidewalk outside 517 Gold was too narrow and deep in shadow to accommodate the smokers. They were hanging out on the terrace outside the federal building across the street. I crossed over. These were my people. I wanted to join them and enter their cloud, but I began to gag on the smoke. I popped another herbal cough drop, well on my way to getting a Ricola jones.

Eric had found Nancy and they were standing at the sunny end of the patio talking intensely to one another as if they were the only two people in the world. Nancy extended her hand. Eric took it. Their linked arms made a long shadow in the afternoon sun. Eric saw me first and dropped Nancy's hand.

"I'm glad that's over with," he said.

"Me, too," I replied.

"How'd we do?" asked Nancy.

"You were perfect," I said.

The Barkers drove back to the East Mountains. After work I went to the South Valley to see if I could find Ramona. The North Valley is making the transition from rural Hispanic to rich Anglo. Usually on the outskirts of a growing city only the rich can afford to be rural, but the South Valley hadn't been making that transition yet.

Like Mirador, Sunset Court is a mix of cinder-block houses, mobile homes, and an occasional old adobe. I wondered if this was an Indian neighborhood, although in my experience Albuquerque doesn't have Indian neighborhoods. We have white neighborhoods and brown neighborhoods, but none that I know of that are specifically Indian. Sandia Pueblo is on the north side of the city and Isleta on the south. The people who live there and work in town are close enough to go home at night. Other Native Americans seem to be scattered around town like the rest of us nonnatives.

It was early evening, the sun was casting a long shadow, and Sunset's residents were coming home from work. I dodged a couple of kids peddling their bikes in a demon frenzy, their elbows and knees poking into the street. I saw an old woman walking her dog. She shuffled along in her little-old-lady shoes, but her dog, a rust-colored, thick-maned Chow, had the dainty step and erect bearing of a king. The homes were close together on Sunset, but houses are close together in the Heights, too, and those homes are four thousand square feet. If I had the money myself I'd put it into distance. Many of the places on Sunset had five or six vehicles parked in the driveway and the yard. None of the vehicles were new and most of them were junkers.

Ramona's home, a trailer near the end of the block, had a tiny yard with a chain-link fence surrounding it. There weren't any cars or trucks parked in the street or the yard, which had been scraped bare except for one carefully tended rosebush. The Valley is the rare place in Albuquerque where it takes an effort to keep the vegetation away. If you don't pay attention here, your yard will fill up with sumac, Chinese elm shoots, and Russian thistle that grows round and fat until winter, when it blows loose from its moorings and turns into footloose tumbleweed. I'd hate to think I'm one of those people who tries to re-create childhood wherever she goes, but I do feel an attraction to the big trees and thick weeds that grow along the Valley's irrigation ditches. Maybe Ramona's bare yard reminded her of the Rez. Maybe she'd made an effort to re-create the space.

The curtains in the trailer's windows were shut tight. A child's car seat and pink stuffed animal lay under the steps that led to the door. "No one home," the place whispered, but I parked my car, went to the door, and knocked anyway. There was no answer. Henry Ortega's card protruded from a crack beside the door. I placed one of my own cards next to Henry's. On it I'd written "Thank you, Ramona. We need to talk. Call me." As I turned to walk down the steps the man next door, who'd been watering his patch of green with a garden hose, noticed me. His belly hung out from beneath his undershirt and slopped over his belt buckle. His lawn was surrounded by a white metal fence full of curls and loops. In the middle of the lawn sat a statue of the Virgin of Guadalupe. This man was going to as much trouble to keep his place green as Ramona had taken to make hers empty.

"She's not home," he said.

"Do you know where she is?" I asked.

"No."

"Can you tell me how long she's been gone?"

"Couple of days."

He went back to his watering. I went home and called Mike Marshall.

14

"How'd the interview with the Barkers go?" Mike asked me.

"Okay." Maybe even better than okay. "When is your interview scheduled?"

"Tomorrow."

"I stopped at Ramona's place and found nobody there. Sheila McGraw's still looking for her. She tracked down her mother on the reservation. Mrs. Franklin told Sheila that Ramona left her daughter there and that you picked Ramona up to take her to Thunder Mountain."

"That's right. I did."

"Mrs. Franklin told Sheila that Ramona called the trading post and left a message that she'd come back for her daughter in a few days. Mrs. Franklin said she thought Ramona was in Albuquerque. Ramona didn't take her car to Thunder Mountain, did she?"

"No. She went with me in the Subaru."

"If she's not on the reservation, do you have any idea where she is? Where could she have gone without a car?"

"She and Joni had a friend, Jackie, somewhere near Oro, I think. You could try calling there. Let me see if I still have the number." There was a pause, then he came back on the line. "Oh, yeah. Here it is: 970-555-1240."

I thanked him, hung up, and dialed the number, wondering if that was Jacki with an "i" like Joni. I also wondered if the friend was another female hotshot.

"Hello," Ramona answered in her soft, even voice. There was a buzz on the line coming from either the radio station down my street or a cell phone on the other end.

"This is Neil. Are you all right?" I asked.

"I'm okay. I've been staying up here with my friend."

"You saved my life, Ramona. I don't know how to thank you for that."

"I'm glad I could do it."

"The fire was caused by arson, you know."

There was a pause while she drew in her breath. "Oh, no."

"Sheila McGraw, the arson investigator for the Forest Service, has been looking for you."

Ramona's sigh had wings as it flew from Colorado to the North Valley.

"I'm not your lawyer, but if I were, my advice would be to come back to town immediately. The longer you stay away, the worse it looks."

"All right," she said. "I will be back."

"Where are you anyway?"

"Cloud."

"Could you get here in time to meet me for lunch tomorrow?"

"Yes."

"How 'bout Garcia's on Fourth Street at one o'clock?"

"Okay," she said.

The Fourth Street Garcia's is the Kid's favorite Albuquerque restaurant. Garcia's is all over town now, but this one's the original and he likes the family photos on the walls, the rattlesnake skin from the Valley of Fires that hangs above the door, the red booths, the Formica tabletops, the Mexican food. The waitresses wear dresses with ruffled tops and peasant skirts and they are not little women. On a smaller woman the frills might be too cute, but the waitresses in Garcia's have the dignity to pull it off. No one ever told them they had to be anorexic to be attractive.

Ramona was waiting for me in a booth looking subdued in her faded jeans and work shirt. She stood up and extended her hand, which felt cool and smooth inside mine. Today's special was *chiles rellenos* and we both ordered it.

While we waited for the food I told her the story of the Garcias' son. "He was killed in a traffic accident when he was about eleven or twelve," I said. "I think he was riding his bike. His organs were donated and a woman in California got his heart. After the transplant she developed a craving for Mexican food, which she'd never liked before. She tracked down the Garcias and came to the restaurant to have a Mexican meal and to thank them."

Ramona nodded. "The heart carries a person's feelings," she said.

There were a bundle of feelings in my heart, but gratitude was at the top of the heap. "When I was a child my father used to roll me tight in my blanket when he put me to bed. He called it wrapping me up Indian-style. I remembered that when you put the fire shelter around me."

"We know how to take care of people. You were in good black. I knew you would be safe as long as you stayed inside the shelter."

"When I passed out I saw my father waiting for me at the bottom of a mountain."

"I think he loved you very much. My father loved me but he didn't always show it."

"Mike told me you went to the mountain to leave a tribute to Joni."

"We always leave something at a fire; sometimes it's only a pile of stones. I went back to do that."

"It must have been hard to go back."

"It was."

"You were carrying a fully equipped pack?"

"Yes. It was a tribute to them." I didn't ask Ramona what tribute she'd left on the mountain that day; that seemed more private than relevant.

"I thought I could hear voices when I was in the South Canyon," I said.

"I heard them, too."

"When the trees were burning on the east side I heard

them snap and hiss." The survivor part of me needed to share what I'd experienced with Ramona. We were different in many ways, but we were women. We had survived the loss of our fathers. We had survived fire. Ramona's calmness went deep; it made me want to confide in her.

"They do that," she said.

The food arrived and we stopped talking and concentrated on the *chiles rellenos,* which were hot enough to keep my attention focused. When we finished eating I resumed my questions, which might have been rude but I had to do it. Gratitude wasn't the only feeling in my heart. If nothing else, there's always curiosity pumping.

"Mike Marshall told me he didn't see or talk to you again after you went to leave your tribute."

"No, he didn't," she said. If they were covering for each other, they were sticking to their story.

"Did you see the Barkers or anybody else on the mountain before or during the fire?"

She looked down at her fork, pushing cheese and chile around her plate with a slow circular motion. "No," she mumbled into the plate.

Ramona's pain was so acute that questioning her felt like touching a burned tree and coming away with char all over my hand. "She saved your life," said one of the voices in my heart. "Tom Hogue died. Someone put your life in danger and your clients at risk," said a couple of the others. "Where were you when the fire started?" I asked.

"I was near the top of the mountain. I made my way

into the black and came down through it. I was afraid you
and Mike were still up there."

"Did you hear the helicopter when it came back?"

"Yes, but I didn't see it land."

"Did Mike tell you that Hogue threatened to fire you?"
I asked.

Ramona looked away from the plate and toward the
wall, where she studied the fiestas, weddings, and gradua-
tions of the Garcia family. "Yes," she said. "I called him
last night after I talked to you."

"Can you tell me why you saved me and not Tom
Hogue?"

"I heard your voice. I heard you coughing. I didn't hear
him. I only had one shelter," she said. "Even if I had heard
him I would have saved you. You work for her family.
You are connected to her."

I wondered again if saving me could compensate in any
way for losing Joni. "I don't know how to tell you how
grateful I am," I said. "I can't be your lawyer because I am
already representing the Barkers, but if there's anything
else I can do for you or your daughter . . . ?"

"We're okay."

"Being a hotshot must mean a lot to you."

"It does. Everyone says it's a big deal to be a point
woman, but all I wanted was to be a firefighter. The crew
boss hired me because I could do the work."

"Was the crew boss in the South Canyon, too?"

She shook her head. "He quit the Forest Service," she said.

"What about you?" I asked. "Are you still planning to
continue? Mike feels he's ruined as a firefighter."

"I have to," she said.

"I can recommend a lawyer."

"I don't need one."

It wasn't much, but she did let me pay for the lunch. I didn't see her vehicle. It was parked in the lot behind the building. Mine was on the street. "Promise me you'll call Sheila McGraw," I said.

"Sure," she said.

"And you'll keep in touch?"

She nodded, but I suspected that if I ever saw Ramona Franklin again I'd be the one to track her down.

Anna was out when I returned to the office. The telephone message light was blinking, but I ignored it, went into my office, and took out the picture of Joni with the snakes wrapped round her arms. In Navajo sand paintings snakes represent lightning, a power that zigzags from the gods to the ground. Lightning strikes suddenly and without warning. Snakes coil before they strike, but it can come without warning if you don't know they're there. It's the nature of fire to get out of control, but all fires go out eventually with or without intervention, I thought. There's more power in starting a fire than there is in putting it out.

15

On Sunday morning I woke with a craving that only *menudo* could fill. The Kid, who was in my bed again, woke up with a craving that only I could fill. It was something else to be grateful to Ramona for—that there were still desires that could be filled. The Kid drifted off to sleep again. I punched his shoulder. "You awake?" I asked.

"I am now."

"Let's go out for *menudo*."

"Why?"

"I like *menudo*." For me it's comfort food, the Mexican version of chicken soup.

He made a face. "You know what *menudo* is?"

"Sure. Cow's stomach." AKA tripe. I was no stranger to tripe. I'd eaten pepper pot soup when I was a kid. Maybe that's when I started making the connection between comfort and spice. It took awhile for science to catch up, but now scientists agree and have their own theory. People in hot climates don't eat chiles simply to hide the taste of rancid meat. Hot peppers contain capsaicin, which stimulates the release of endorphins into the brain to produce a natural high. You have to do something to disguise tripe. On its own it's slimy as a snail, but add some *posole* and red chile and it'll start your engine.

"Why you want to eat that?" the Kid asked.

"Why not? You eat *chicharrones*." AKA fried pork fat, also high on the unappealing scale.

"That's different."

The only difference I could see was that *chicharrones* were crunchy and *menudo* was not. "Let's go to PJ's," I said. "You can get a *chicharrones* burrito there."

"Okay," he said, getting out of bed and looking around for something to wear. "Where's my shirt, Chiquita?"

"Which one?"

"The red one."

"In the closet."

He opened the closet door and said, *"Híjole,"* when he saw how much space his clothes were taking up. "I have a lot of stuff here." He took the red shirt from the hanger and put it on. "This is a nice house, Chiquita. I like it here."

"Let's go to breakfast," I said.

The only place in New Mexico I'd eat the *menudo* more than once is PJ's. In most places it's more rubber than flavor. PJ's is a small café with a big parking lot that even on Sunday morning is never full. The Kid chomped his burrito while I slurped my *menudo*. I finished with three cups of coffee and had enough of a caffeine and capsaicin buzz to get me where I wanted to go, which was not back to my unorganized house. The Kid didn't have any plans for the afternoon, I knew, but tomorrow was another story.

"Do you have a busy day tomorrow?" I asked him.

He shrugged. "*Mas o menos.* Why?"

"I was thinking it might be interesting to go up to Colorado."

"Where in Colorado?"

"Thunder Mountain."

"Why do you want to do that?" The Kid had cleaned his plate and put down his knife and fork.

"The Forest Service has finished their investigation and they're opening the area up again today. I'd like to see if I can find anything they missed. I'd like to see who goes back."

"That's it?"

"I'd kind of like to see it again myself." I also wanted to show him the place where I'd nearly burned to death, but I didn't say that. "Do you have anything to do tomorrow that Rafael couldn't handle?"

"Not really," he said. "What about your office?"

"Nothing major."

"Okay," he said. "*Vamos.*"

We took the Hispanic road this time and made it to Thunder Mountain in four hours. Across from the road into the campground was a large wooden sign that read "Mountain View Estates—Ten-Acre Lots for Sale." A hawk had been carved into the sign and was winging it above the letters. Several houses inhabited a grassy meadow, but there was room for several more. The houses were variations on a theme: view-oriented, rustic, with roofs made out of cedar shakes. It was a planned development—too planned for me. The houses looked up the East Canyon toward the peak of Thunder Mountain. Until recently the view must have been spectacular, but now the burn mark was a black snake slithering across the mountain with charred tree trunks standing watch on the ridge top. There was new black among the old black, but from here there was no way of telling where one ended and the other began. I asked the Kid to pull over.

"See the burn up there? That's where I was," I said.

"You are very lucky you survived that, Chiquita."

"I know." And I had the cough to prove it.

The top of the mountain was a stark reminder of the awesome power of fire, but much of the drainage area was still green. I directed the Kid toward the campground. Thick arms of cottonwoods shaded the road. Squirrels raced up the trunks and darted across the branches.

"From here it looks like nothing happened," the Kid said.

But near here was where it had all started. "It's deceptive," I replied.

We parked in the parking lot, got out, and walked to the cottonwood where the Barkers had waited. Either they'd left nothing behind or the area had been thoroughly scoured by investigators. There was no sign they'd been here, no sign this area had ever been an encampment, no fusees or other fire-fighting equipment lying on the ground. Trails wandered behind the parking lot and the Kid and I took the one that headed north. At first it was so quiet you could hear the leaves fall. Then I heard the sound of chattering birds that, as they got closer, turned out to be hikers, two women around sixty wearing floppy hats, shorts, and hiking boots. Binoculars dangled from their necks. Birders. I'd know them anywhere. Wisps of gray hair slipped out from under their hats. One had long, skinny legs and the hunched shoulders of a woman who'd always felt she was too tall. The other was shorter with a round butt.

"Hello," one called.

"Good morning," said the other.

"Hi," I replied, stopping to chat. "Seen any birds?"

"A few," the taller woman said.

"This is the first time they let us back after the fire," added her companion. "We haven't seen anybody else hiking yet."

"We're not exactly hiking," I replied.

"No?" The shorter woman had the bright eyes and musical voice of a wren. It trilled up the scale and pinged back down. Every word had a couple of notes and every sentence a melody.

"I survived the blaze," I said.

They were suitably impressed. "Wow," the wren chirped.

"You did?" The taller woman looked down as she talked and her head bobbed like a crane searching for fish. "I watched that fire through my picture window. It was fierce."

"Do you live in Mountain View Estates?" It would be a convenient place for bird-watching, and, lately, fire watching.

"Yes, I do."

"Did you glass the fire?" I asked. I'd picked up birder talk from my Aunt Joan.

"I did, but all I could see was smoke and flames. I never saw any people, but I heard a Forest Service employee died up there."

"That's right."

"What were you doing on Thunder Mountain that day?" asked the wren.

"I'm a lawyer representing the family of one of the hotshots who was killed in the South Canyon. We flew in to look at the site. A Forest Service official and I got caught in the fire on the way down. I made it out; he didn't."

"We were birding in the drainage that day and we heard the helicopter taking off and landing," the crane said. "It sounded like a war zone."

"It's hard to ignore a helicopter," I agreed.

"You were lucky you survived. *Very* lucky," said the wren.

"I know." The Kid had heard all this before and was poking at the ground with his running shoe. If he was wondering how much mileage I intended to get out of my part in the fire, the answer was as much as would help me uncover the cause.

"If it hadn't been for us they'd have let the South Canyon fire burn," the crane said.

"Really?" I asked.

"Really. When I heard about it I got on the phone and called my senator and my representative. And Emily"—she nodded at her friend—"called the head of the Colorado office of the BLM."

"You know those people?" I asked.

"Every one of 'em," she said. "We're on the board of the Colorado Audubon Society. We vote. We contribute to political campaigns. I'm not going to sit by and wait for my house to go up in smoke."

"Who would?" I wondered. Few people—no matter how environmentally aware—would let their own house burn, unless, of course, there was an ulterior motive.

Emily trilled, "The slurry bombers roared through the valley right above Margaret's house. We were standing outside. If they'd known we were the ones who called, they might have dropped the slurry on top of us!" She laughed.

"That fire would have burned itself out eventually," I said. Some houses might have been lost, but lives would have been saved.

"We wanted to be sure," Emily said.

"You said you were in the drainage the afternoon of the second fire?"

"We were birding, but when we smelled the smoke we drove to Margaret's house and got on the phone again."

"Did you see anybody else here that day?" I asked. Birders, after all, are known for their sharp eyes.

"We saw a hiker sitting under the cottonwood tree," Margaret, the crane, said.

"Male or female?"

"Female. A young blond woman."

"How young?"

"Forty-five?" Emily asked.

"Fifty," Margaret replied.

"Was she alone?"

"Yes."

"Did she have a pack with her?"

"I didn't see one," Margaret answered.

"Did you see any cars in the parking lot?"

"A red compact."

"And we saw the brown truck," Emily said.

"That's right. Driving like a bat out of hell. We've seen vehicles before on the old logging road. After Thunder Mountain was declared a wilderness area, all vehicles were banned from entering the forest and from ever using the logging road. They should have bulldozed it shut, but they never got around to doing it. If the Forest Service catches a vehicle in a wilderness area, the owner has to disassemble it and have it towed out by horses. Technically, even flying the firefighters in was a violation, but we didn't say anything about that, did we, Em?"

"No, we didn't."

"What kind of license plate did the truck have? Did you notice?" I asked.

"Colorado," Margaret said.

"Was the person driving it a man or a woman?"

"Couldn't tell. Could you?"

"No, but he or she wore a cowboy hat," Emily said.

The Kid was looking longingly down the lonesome trail. I only had one more question and that was "How do you feel about the spotted owl?"

"We believe in the preservation of species through the preservation of habitat," Emily said.

"Absolutely," Margaret agreed. "We're members of Forest Sentinels. We monitor the Forest Service to make sure they uphold the Endangered Species Act."

"Go for it," I said.

"See you later," said the Kid.

A squirrel bitched as we continued down the sun-dappled path. We were intruders on its turf, but we left it behind, following a yellow butterfly that darted in and out of the shadows like a flying flicker of flame. The trees began to show char on their northern side. I stopped to examine the thick, scaly bark of an alligator juniper. When I touched the bark it crumbled and tinged my fingers black. Some fluke of fuel, wind, or fusees had kept the fire here from burning with the intensity it had higher up. Green trees mingled with black snags and trees that had partially burned. A tiny pink flower bloomed at the base of a half-dead piñon. The yellow butterfly flew as far as an upended cottonwood, fluttered around the root system, and turned back. We kept going until there were no flowers blooming, until we were surrounded by char and ashes, by good black, safe black, black without the potential to reburn—except in my memory and my dreams. My heart skipped a beat. All the oxygen seemed to have been depleted from the air. I was getting light-headed. We were stepping on ashes, stirring up ghosts. I'd gone about as far as I wanted to go.

"You want to continue, Chiquita?" the Kid asked.

"No. Let's get out of here."

When we reached the parking lot, the big sky opened up. I watched the clouds drifting into the shapes of fingers and mouths. One cloud formed an **S** curve, reminding me that, for a firefighter, lightning can be dollar signs in the sky. But firefighters, I knew, weren't the only ones with the potential to profit from fire.

"Let's drive up the mountain. There was a house there and I'd like to see what's left."

"Okay," said the Kid.

16

We turned north as we left the parking lot, driving through the green area, then the burn. After about a mile the road swung east, leaving the drainage and climbing uphill. I figured this was the place where a wilderness gate had prohibited motorbikes from entering and where the sign marked the area as forbidden to all motorized vehicles, but the gate and the sign had gone up in smoke. Somewhere around here the old logging road had cut through the forest, but that path was hidden by fallen trees and ash. Would an arsonist have driven in and taken the risk of a severe penalty? Why not just hide the truck beside the road, walk in, and run out? But that was assuming the person in the cowboy hat who drove the brown truck like a bat out of hell was an arsonist. The driver could just as well have been a witness or someone trying to escape from the blaze and report it to the Forest Service.

The road up to the house, which crossed private land, had been cleared of dead trees. It was well maintained but steep, and the Kid had to downshift to climb around the curves. The fire had been ruinous to this portion of the forest. The trunks left standing belonged to ponderosa pines, and it was easy to imagine fire jumping from crown to crown to cedar-shake roof. It was harder to imagine fire engines chugging their way up here like the little engine that could. Anyone who lived on this steep, remote road expecting to be safe from fire was California dreaming.

We came around a curve and upon the remains of the trophy house. The pile of black beams and ashes was a sight to drive a stake through any homeowner's heart.

Even the Kid was taken aback. "What a disaster!" he said.

The only thing left standing was a massive stone fireplace with a chimney pointing up. The foundation could have easily accommodated most of the houses on my block. I tried to visualize how this place had been furnished before it burned down. Big leather sofas, I figured, Navajo rugs, and wooden coyotes with scarves tied round their necks. The privacy was complete, the view had to have been magnificent before it got scarred by the burn. A black Bronco was parked in the driveway and a tall, skinny man stood beside it staring at the remains of his multi-thousand-square-foot trophy. He wore Reeboks and Ray-Bans. His gray hair was slicked back into a ponytail. A silver ear cuff was wrapped around the edge of one ear. I would have guessed Santa Fe if I hadn't known California. I'd seen this dude before on Nancy Barker's tape of the Kyle Johnson interview. He was the guy who'd mouthed off about the government's responsibility to protect private property.

The Kid was already looking in the rearview mirror. "What do you want to do?" he asked me.

"Talk to him," I said.

"Okay, I wait here."

"Okay," I said, stepping out of the truck.

The property owner approached to within a few feet of us. He raised his Ray-Bans and I could see that his eyes were the same brittle blue as the turquoise in his ear cuff. "This is private property," he said.

"Are you Ken Roland?" I asked.

"How did you know that?"

"I saw you on TV," I said, figuring that would soften him up. Anybody who'd build a house this large would have to have an ego to match.

"Channel 7 or 12?" he asked.

"Twelve," I said. "Kyle Johnson."

"Asshole," he mumbled.

"Excuse me?"

"The guy's an asshole. He was on my case about the urban/wildland interface. I'm sorry those firefighters died, but hey, it wasn't my fault."

"You did build kind of close to a wilderness area. I hear the local property owners put a lot of pressure on the Forest Service to put that fire out."

"Would you just sit back and watch your house burn?"

"Probably not." But I couldn't afford to live at the edge of the wilderness either. I had a job and an office to get to most days.

"I'm on a county road. I pay taxes. I believe that entitles me to fire protection," Roland said.

In theory, maybe, but in reality the nearest fire engine had to be twenty miles away. He'd built a house with a wooden roof at the edge of a vast and frequently bone-dry forest, and wildland firefighters are not trained to put out house fires. He wasn't the first western settler to want all the privileges of owning private property with none of the obligations.

"The Forest Service wouldn't let me back in until today."

"They were conducting an investigation," I said.

"So I've been told. Great site here, wasn't it?" he asked.

"It was." Until he began looking at charred trees. "How far down the mountain did the first fire burn?" I asked him.

"About a third of the way."

"That must have spoiled your view."

"It did. I used to like to sit out on the deck in my hot tub and watch the sunset. It's no fun to be looking at destruction. This place developed a bad vibe for me after the firefighters died."

How inconsiderate of them, I thought. "Are you planning to rebuild?"

"I doubt it. It'll be a long time before this canyon grows back to what it was. I loved this place, but it was isolated. I'm thinking of moving closer to town."

"Oro?"

"Telluride," he said, where the median house goes for a cool million. A large insurance settlement would help if he intended to buy there.

"Did you come here from California?" I asked.

"Yeah."

"A native?"

"How'd you know that?"

"An educated guess." Some Californians are always ready to move on, always searching for the perfect place. That type wouldn't sit around waiting for the trees to grow.

"What'd you say your name was?" Ken Roland's eyes narrowed like they were seeing me for the first time. He'd been too busy talking about himself to pay any attention to whom he was talking.

"Neil Hamel," I said. A cough was crawling up the back of my throat. I tried to suppress it, but I didn't succeed.

"What brings you up here?"

"I'm thinking about buying at Mountain View," I said, proving to myself that I could lie and cough at the same time. "I'm worried about the forest fire danger and I wanted to prepare myself for the worst. It's got to be agonizing to watch your house burn down." But when you think about it, maybe less agonizing to a native Californian. It happens all the time there. Roland himself seemed more annoyed than agonized about the loss of his trophy.

"It helps to have good insurance, but I wouldn't build at Mountain View if I were you. That's a retirement community. You're too young for Mountain View," he said, sizing me up from dusty running shoes to messy hair.

"Not that young," I said, and coughed to prove it.

"You ought to quit smoking."

"Right," I replied. "I'll be needing a good policy if I do

build at Mountain View. Could you recommend an insurance agent?"

"Sure. His name is Jim Capshaw; Capshaw Insurance in Oro. He's done all right by me."

A woman had stepped out from behind the fireplace and was picking her way carefully across the fallen beams. Her hair was very long and very blond. She wore shorts, a T-shirt, and cowboy boots.

"This is Karen," Roland said. "Karen, Neil. Neil, Karen."

"Pleasure to meet you," I said.

"Hi," said Karen. Her eyes were red and mascara was running down her cheeks.

"It's just a house, Karen," Roland said. "I can build another one."

"I loved it here." She sobbed. "It was so peaceful and quiet. The deer would practically eat out of my hand."

"Karen is an animal lover," Roland said.

"It was horrible when the fire burned," she continued. "The hawks were circling overhead waiting for the animals to escape from the flames. I watched it from the deck."

"She wouldn't leave till the last minute," Roland said. "She stood on the deck with the garden hose spraying down the roof."

"You were here when the fire started?" I asked Karen.

She nodded. "I was sick and I came home early from work. I'm a waitress at Winter's. Ken was in town. The fire was a wall of flame and it came up so fast. It was terrifying. I tried to save the house."

Ken put his arm around her and began rubbing his hand up and down her bare arm.

"I love it here. I love the woods," Karen said.

"Where are you from?" I asked.

"Kansas. Ken and I met when I was ski-bumming at Aspen."

The Kid's patience had run out and he started the engine. "I gotta go," I said.

"Adios," Ken Roland said.

17

We spent the night in a motel on the highway outside Oro where the tractor trailers barrel through all night. It could have been New Mexico, it could have been New Jersey. The bedspread was shiny and smooth. The rust-colored carpet was so shaggy you'd need a Weedwacker to level it. The drinking glasses were wrapped tight in plastic, the ice bucket made of Styrofoam. It was the kind of room that some people find sterile and stifling but I used to call home. You could be anywhere in a room like this. You could be anybody. The TV was at the foot of the bed and the remote was on the end table. The Kid lay down on the bed and clicked the TV on.

I went to the bathroom and when I came back the Kid was watching baseball, which I find about as exciting as watching a praying mantis climb the wall.

"Good game?" I asked.

"It's okay."

"Who's winning?"

"Braves."

It took about five minutes for the ball game to put me to sleep. Some time after that it put the Kid out, too. The game was followed by news and later by snow. I know that because I woke up a couple of times looking for the remote to turn the thing off but it had gotten lost among the sheets. The screen was a change from what I'd been dreaming about anyway—fire and smoke.

In the morning we had breakfast at the McDonald's in Oro. The Kid let me off downtown, took the truck, and went looking for Oscar Ribera, a guy he'd known in Mexico who was working the Colorado ski business. I walked down Main Street looking for Jim Capshaw.

There's a kind of surreal clarity in these Rocky Mountain high towns. Oro has the solid brick buildings and busy main street of an old western town and the latte bars of a new tourist town. The small towns in this part of Colorado are isolated enough to still have independent bookstores. Oro has Maria's. It looked interesting, but it wasn't open yet, and besides, I had work to do. I found Capshaw's office in a brick building with a half-moon window looking down on Main Street. He had a large oak desk, wooden file cabinets, and a musty antlered deer head mounted on the wall. There was probably a time when you wouldn't have been able to get an insurance policy in Oro in hunting season, but that was before the Old West became the new and the big money started moving in. It took me a while to figure out where Jim Capshaw figured in the old/new scheme. He was a burly guy with dark hair forming spirals on his arms and whirlpools on his chest. He wore a short-sleeved plaid shirt open at the collar, cowboy boots, and Wranglers, known in New Mexico as big-ass jeans. Levi's are popular with new Westerners, but Wranglers are the jeans old cowboys wear; there's more room in the butt. Were the Wranglers a calculated move on Capshaw's part or had he grown up among cowboys? He had the kind of folksiness you'd expect from a small-town insurance agent, but he didn't overdo it.

"Jim Capshaw," he said, extending his arm across the pool-table–sized desk.

I reached over and shook his hand. "Neil Hamel," I said.

"I had an uncle named Neil."

"So did I."

"What can I do you for?" he asked.

"I'm thinking about buying a lot in Mountain View," I told him.

"Great development," he answered with an enthusiasm that made me wonder if he wasn't a partner.

"It's a beautiful spot."

"Sure is."

"But I'm worried about the danger of forest fires."

"Well, we've had two this summer and Mountain View escaped both of 'em. We couldn't be unlucky enough to have another for a long time. The next time lightning strikes, it'll hit someplace else."

"I took a ride up to see Ken Roland's place. It's nothing but a pile of ashes. I'd hate to see my house end up like that."

"It's a tragedy, all right," Capshaw agreed, "but Ken wasn't hurt and he did have good coverage."

"He recommended you."

"That was neighborly of him."

"Do you live near Thunder Mountain?"

"No, but I like to think of everybody in the county as my neighbor. It's getting harder these days, but I keep trying."

"Does Ken intend to rebuild?" I asked.

"Far as I know."

"I hope he'll use a metal roof the next time."

"It would be better from an insurance standpoint," Capshaw concurred. "When you get a fire of that magnitude, being in the next county could have saved Ken's house but a metal roof wouldn't have made any difference."

"Are wildland firefighters available to protect houses?"

"That depends on the BLM and the Forest Service. Their firefighters aren't really trained to fight house fires and the Feds won't be so quick to call 'em out after the South Canyon incident, but you won't have to worry about that at Mountain View. Those houses aren't in the woods and, like I said, I don't think we're gonna get another fire in this area for a long while."

"Would I get a better rate if I cleared out the brush and used a metal roof? You do better where I live in Albuquerque if you install a burglar alarm."

"We may be headed in that direction," Capshaw said, "but it hasn't happened yet. You wouldn't be able to use a metal roof at Mountain View anyway. The restrictive covenants limit the roofing to cedar shake."

"I've heard rumors that the fire that burned Ken Roland's house down was caused by arson."

Light darted from one of Capshaw's eyes to the other like lightning jumping from cloud to cloud. Small towns are always full of rumors and I figured he'd heard every one of them. Fire, after all, was his business. He paused for a moment to consider what was good for that business, whether Oro's expansion would be threatened more by a natural disaster or one that was man-made. He came down on the side of the natural. Man-made disasters were what everybody was moving here to get away from. "Arson? That's news to me," he said.

"Karen told me that Ken insured his truck through you, too. Maybe you could handle my Nissan."

"Karen? Do I know a Karen?" Capshaw's thick eyebrows formed a caterpillar arc.

"She's Ken's girlfriend."

"I thought *her* name was Deb."

"Straight blond hair? Long legs? Early twenties?"

"Nah, Deb's a redhead. She does have great legs. I guess that goes with owning a ten-thousand-square-foot house." He laughed. "What were you sayin' about a truck?"

"Karen told me you insured Ken's truck." The lie was getting smoother with practice. The words were rolling off my tongue like polished gemstones.

"Ken doesn't own a truck. I insure him for his Blazer and his Ferrari."

"Where does he get all his money from anyway?"

"Venture capital. He invested heavily in Silicon Valley.

161

There's a guy who can live anywhere he wants with anybody he pleases. Give these guys a modem and a cell phone and they can work anywhere. That's what's fueling Oro's expansion."

I knew enough about venture capital and the computer business to know that sometimes you win big and sometimes you lose even bigger. Ken Roland might have been on a losing streak and needed the money a fire would bring in. The South Canyon fire had to have decreased the value of his house, but he did have good insurance, making it more profitable, perhaps, to burn than to sell.

"I suppose he has a large mortgage to pay off," I said.

"No mortgage," Capshaw said. "It was a cash deal. Guys like him are reshaping the West. They've got the money to turn these small Colorado towns around. Ninety thousand Californians moved into Colorado last year. I figure you can fight 'em or you can join 'em."

It was good for the economy, bad for the sense of community. How you felt about the growth depended on how badly you needed the money, how much you cared about preserving the place you lived. There's a lot of resistance to change in the rural West, enough even to make me wonder if Ken Roland's house might have been torched by someone other than Ken Roland. "How do they feel about newcomers around here?"

"Depends on where you're from." Capshaw grinned, straddling the line between real honesty and good business. Sometimes honesty works for you in business, sometimes not. "Are you from California?"

"New Mexico," I said.

"That's right. You mentioned that, didn't you?"

"Yeah."

"You'll have no problem," he replied. "You'll love Oro." New Mexicans are welcome most places; we're not rich enough or numerous enough to threaten anybody's way of life.

"You have a chapter of Forest Sentinels here?" It was the environmental group the birders had said they belonged to. Forest Sentinels was active in New Mexico and, in fact, was embroiled in controversy because loggers believed the environmentalists were preventing them from making a living.

"Well, yeah, we have a chapter, but you wouldn't want to be involved with them."

"Why not?"

"They're troublemakers," Jim Capshaw said.

"Well, thanks for your help," I said. "I'll let you know if I decide to buy at Mountain View."

"You do that."

I bumped the nose of the deer on my way out and raised a cloud of dust. "Getting a little musty," I said.

"I'm thinking of taking it down," Capshaw replied.

18

The Kid and I had agreed to reconnoiter at two, which left me plenty of time to track down the Forest Sentinels' office in a ramshackle Victorian house several blocks south of Main Street. The woman sitting at the reception desk had a fair amount of gray hair among the blond, but the hairdo was youthful—long and curly. She wore jeans and a Guatemalan *huipil* with embroidery all over it. She was older than many of the people I'd been talking to lately, but equally fit. On her desk sat several mugs with dangling strings of tea bags. The sun beamed in through a bay window, making it brilliantly clear that the walls of the office needed painting, the floor needed sanding, and the curtains were ragged. Environmental organizations tend to have minimal funding for office and staff. The woman might have been a receptionist, but my guess was she ran the place. This office felt like her nest. There were a couple of rooms behind her, but I couldn't see who or what was in them. The posters of green forests tacked to the walls and the framed photographs on her desk were bright and shiny spots in the shabby room. Another woman might have had pictures of her lover or her children; she had pictures of a wolf. I've never seen a wolf that wasn't magnificent myself. This one was sitting, standing, howling, sleeping. In one memorable shot its paws were on the woman's shoulders and it stared her in the face.

I know a wolf when I see one, but just to get her reaction I said, "Nice dog."

"It's not a dog," the woman replied. "It's a wolf."

"What's its name?"

"Savage. Can I help you with something?"

"Maybe," I replied, segueing into the lie that had been working so far. "I'm from New Mexico and thinking about moving up here. I'm trying to get a feel for the place."

"Forest Sentinels has a chapter in Santa Fe."

"I know."

I also knew that their leader had recently been burned in effigy by loggers who felt Forest Sentinels' support of spotted owl habitat was costing loggers their jobs. I like forests and I didn't necessarily disagree with Forest Sentinels' goals, but my purpose here was not to join up, only to gather information.

"I'm sympathetic to what you're doing, but it would be nice to get away from controversy," I said.

She laughed, showing spaces between her teeth. This woman didn't have the look of pampered privilege common to many environmentalists. She did have the determined look of someone who'd found a calling in midlife. "It's getting hard to avoid controversy in the West nowadays," she said.

"True," I replied. "So tell me what you guys are all about. What's your mission in Oro?"

"Preserving forests. Preserving wildlife habitat. Trying to prevent the Forest Service from caving in to ranchers, loggers, and other special interest groups. Many of our members are former Forest Service employees. We think the government's policy of fire suppression is a disaster. The forests were a lot healthier when fires were left to burn out naturally. Nowadays fuel buildup has turned Western forests into a tinderbox. The fires are bigger and hotter than they've ever been."

"So the idea is to save forests by letting them burn?" I asked.

"In the long run. In the meantime we advocate controlled burns."

"You've had a couple of forest fires nearby, I hear."

"Right, and nine firefighters were killed unnecessarily."

"What do you think the Forest Service should have done in the South Canyon?"

"Let it burn," she said, looking me right in the eye. She wasn't smooth or pretty, but her convictions gave her a certain raw power.

"What about the houses that go up in smoke?"

"As far as I am concerned, they can burn, too."

"Isn't that kind of drastic? People do get attached to their homes."

"Then they shouldn't build near wilderness areas," she replied. Wolves are smart and wary. You'd expect a woman who hung out with them to have a good bullshit detector, but hers seemed to be working overtime. I hadn't asked *that* many questions. Yet already her eyes were narrowing and her shoulders getting hunched and tense.

"Are you a reporter?" she asked.

"No."

"Then why all the questions?"

"Just naturally curious, I guess." It was a weaselly answer and I got a ferret's response.

"What did you say your name was?" she barked.

"I didn't. I have to get going; I'm meeting someone at McDonald's. Thanks for your help."

"Did you find out what you came here for?" she asked.

"More or less," I replied.

Leaving an irritated and suspicious woman behind me at Forest Sentinels, I walked down the street to McDonald's. It was only one o'clock and I still had an hour to kill, so I got myself a Big Mac with fries and sat down near the window to eat and wait for the Kid. It was lunchtime; McDonald's was crowded but not packed. I was just finishing up my hamburger when a guy with a tray in his hands stopped at my table and asked if he could join me. Maybe he thought I was the best-looking woman in the restaurant. Maybe not.

"Have a seat," I said. My dining companion had a narrow

face, a sharp nose, dark shoulder-length hair, and a scrawny build. He moved gingerly, which made him kind of comforting after all the super-fit and athletic people I'd recently met. He put down his tray and picked up his hamburger. He'd sought me out; I let him make the first move.

"You visiting Oro?" he asked in a raspy voice.

"That's right."

"How do you like it?"

"It's okay. There seem to be a lot of very fit people in this town."

His smile was thin but appealing. "Is that why you're thinking about moving up here? You want to get in shape?"

"Not really." I'd told my lie about moving to Oro to two people. I put my money on the woman from Forest Sentinels as the person who'd passed it on to him. "You're from Forest Sentinels?" I asked.

He was cutting his fries into tiny pieces and choosing his words with care. "I am affiliated with them."

On what basis? I wondered. He didn't have the polished teeth, rumpled cotton, shiny-haired look of an Ivy League environmentalist. He was wearing black jeans and a black T-shirt. His lank hair fell in front of his face. Maybe Forest Sentinels was reaching out for support, which could be a good thing. Environmentalism doesn't have to be a class struggle. We all stand to lose when the environment gets trashed. Before I could ask what exactly he did for Forest Sentinels I had another coughing fit.

"That's a bad cough," he said.

"It's getting better."

"What are you? Some kind of investigator?"

"I'm a lawyer," I said.

Usually a knee jerks when I name my profession, but this guy just gave me another thin smile. "So why all the curiosity? Forest Sentinels is Ms. O'Connor's baby. She gets uncomfortable when people ask too many questions."

"Has she got something to hide?" I asked.

"No. She's up front."

"She does speak her mind," I said.

"You told her you were from New Mexico?" He brushed his hair back from his face.

"That's right."

"So what are you doing here? Are you representing someone in Oro?" He was asking a fair number of questions himself.

"I can't say; it's a matter of client confidentiality."

"Where is it in New Mexico that you're from? Santa Fe?"

"Albuquerque."

"Albuquerque." He looked out the window, where kids were swinging and sliding on McDonald's multicolored playground. His eyes were dark and sad when they turned back to me. "I've been through some bad times," the eyes said. "I'll take care of you," some women might have answered, but not me and apparently not wolf woman either, or she'd have had his picture on her desk.

"Where'd you get the cough?" he asked.

It must have been all over the Oro news that an Albuquerque lawyer was caught in the East Canyon fire. My cough could have blown my cover, but whether that would matter or not remained to be seen. "I was in a forest fire," I told him.

"Which one?"

"East Canyon."

"That's too bad," he said.

"Isn't it?"

The Kid had appeared in McDonald's doorway looking curly-haired and upbeat. I stood up and waved him over.

"Friend of yours?" my companion asked.

"You could say that."

The guy picked up his tray and prepared to make a getaway.

"What'd you say your name was?" I asked him.

His mouth laughed. His eyes did not. "I didn't," he replied.

"Who was that?" the Kid asked, watching no-name environmentalist maneuver his way through the obstacle course of McDonald's. The Kid's voice had that proprietary tone men get when they think a rival has appeared on the scene. Did the guy have rival potential? I wondered. I thought not; he was too dark and brooding for me.

"He's an environmentalist connected to Forest Sentinels. That's all I know," I replied.

The Kid went to get himself something to eat. I looked out the window to see what kind of vehicle the guy drove away in, but he wasn't driving. He crossed the street and walked slowly up the hill.

"Did you find Oscar Ribera?" I asked the Kid when he returned with his Big Mac.

"Yeah. Did you find the insurance agent?"

"I did and he was very cooperative. I found out that Ken Roland has good insurance. He'll make a lot of money on the ashes of his house."

"Guys like him always make a lot of money, no?"

"Yes. How's Oscar doing?"

He shook his head. "He's living with a bunch of guys in a trailer. It's not so crowded now; there's not much work in the summer and many of the guys go someplace else. In the winter they work in restaurants and hotels and take turns sleeping on the floor. It costs too much to live close to the ski areas. They have to drive far on the snowy roads. They leave in the dark, they come home in the dark. I think it was the right move for me to go to Albuquerque."

"I know it," I said. Business was booming in the Duke City. A good mechanic could make as much as an average lawyer. But the Kid would land on his feet wherever he went.

We cruised by Forest Sentinels on our way out of town, but I didn't see any brown truck parked near the office. We took the Chama route home, stopping for a few minutes at Abiquiu Reservoir, where the Kid wanted to watch the water flow and listen to the wind blow. But after having witnessed the ashes of Ken Roland's house I was anxious to make sure mine was still standing. Adobes don't burn very often, but they can. When we got back to town, the Kid dropped me at my door and went to the shop to check up on Mimo, his parrot.

My house was exactly as I had left it. The kitchen was

still waiting for a backhoe to show up. The Kid's clothes were in the closet. I walked through the house looking at the vigas and the tiles, touching the fireplace and the walls. I never thought it could happen to me, but I was falling in love with a house. Once you've slept in it, had sex in it, been sick in it, then a house becomes a home. It doesn't take long to fill it with memories and stuff. When you torch someone's home, I thought, you turn their soul to ashes. Hard to imagine someone burning up his own home, but people commit suicide often enough.

I walked into the empty room and was standing there when the Kid arrived. He looked at the white walls, the brick floors, the empty *nicho*, mentally filling it up, I knew, but with what? Family? Friends? Guys sleeping on mattresses on the floor? His stuff?

"Are you always going to keep this room empty?" he asked.

"Why not?" I replied. It wasn't a luxury or a necessity— just a kind of clearing like Ramona's yard. She'd had to work to keep her place empty and, so it seemed, would I.

"Mimo gets lonely in the shop at night," the Kid said.

A house also becomes a home when there's a child in residence, but a parrot? "I don't think so," I said.

19

On Tuesday morning I called Sheila McGraw. "How was your weekend?" I asked.

"I had to take my dog to the vet. Otherwise okay. How 'bout you?"

"Interesting. I went back to Thunder Mountain."

I knew what she'd be doing, pushing her glasses back up her nose. "And what did you find there?"

"Ken Roland."

"Oh, him."

"He had a good insurance policy."

"We're checking it out, Neil. A guy who loses an expensive house in a fire is a suspect, and we're looking into his girlfriend Karen, too. She was at Roland's house that afternoon, but she's not a likely suspect; she's an animal lover. The sheriff's deputies had to drag her out of the place kicking and screaming about Bambi. Doesn't it seem unlikely to you that a guy would torch a house with a girlfriend in it?"

"He may not have known she was in it. She told me she didn't feel well and came home from work early."

"Henry's up there this week investigating."

"Roland invests in the computer industry, a risky business. If I had the resources I'd check out his financial situation."

"You lookin' for a job?"

If I was, it wasn't her job. "Just trying to help. I also ran into some birders who were unhappy about the spotted owl situation."

"Names, addresses?"

I had two half names, one partial address, but that would lead to the brown truck and that was a lead I wasn't ready to give up until I knew whether or not it would help my case. "No," I said. "They told me they were members of Forest Sentinels."

"The woods are full of angry people these days. Ranchers, hunters, birders, environmentalists, Forest Sentinels, the Wise Use Movement, you name it. Everybody's pissed and everybody has a different idea of who owns the West. The place is turning into an emotional tinderbox. It's getting so Forest Service employees are afraid to go anywhere in their green rigs, but I still believe the East Canyon fire was an inside job. Whoever started that fire knew what he or she was doing. Ramona Franklin came in voluntarily, by the way."

"Good."

"She's a woman of few words. Less talk than action, I'd say. Henry did better with her than I did. She mentioned you advised her to come in and I want to thank you for that."

"I suggested she get her own lawyer."

"She says she doesn't want a lawyer. She wants to handle this the Indian way. She says she went to the mountain to leave a tribute to Joni Barker and that she was coming down when she saw the fire, heard you screaming, and covered you with her fire shelter. If anybody can tell me what the Indian way is, I'd sure like to know. I hear all this talk about Indians revering fire and suffering when trees go up in smoke, but I've been in the South Dakota office. They started fires up there often enough when they needed powwow money. Supposedly this country was all virgin timber before the white man came and a squirrel could leap from Maine to California without ever touching ground. It's bullshit. The Indians have known how to start fire and have used it for their purposes for a long, long time. Was torching the mountain Ramona's idea of a tribute to the dead firefighters? Is it the Indian way to incinerate a member of the Forest Service because you want to prove a point, or because you bear a grudge, or because he threatens to fire you?

"Excuse me," she said. "I'm thinking out loud."

How did she know about the firing threat? I wondered. Could Mike Marshall have told her? Was she even smarter than I'd given her credit for? I was glad this conversation was taking place over the phone so she couldn't see the expression on my face. It was a Marlboro (or a poor substitute) moment and I was already reaching for the Ricola bag. "Tom Hogue threatened to fire Ramona?" I asked as disingenuously as I was capable of.

"Actually he didn't have the power, but he was mouthing off about it around the Forest Service. Hogue was the old Forest Service. He wasn't known for diplomacy and he had zero respect for women. If you ask me he was the wrong person at the wrong time for the wrong job. The only qualification he had was seniority. It wouldn't surprise me if the things he said made their way back to Ramona. Just because she doesn't talk much doesn't mean she doesn't listen. Don't get me wrong about Indians. They do a great job for the Forest Service, but they keep things to themselves and why not? You can't blame them for not trusting us, can you? But because they're private, they're like a drive-in movie screen that everybody tries to project larger-than-life images on. They weren't savages when we got here and they're not all saints and shamans now. You think about stuff like this when you were given a name like mine. If Ramona set that fire, whatever her reasons for doing it, arson is arson and I'm going to treat her just like any other perp. She was friendly with your clients' daughter, I hear."

"That's right."

"I understand Mrs. Barker blames Ramona and/or the Forest Service for Joni's death and that she has a hot temper."

"Really?" I replied.

"I don't need to remind you, do I," Sheila continued, "that this is an ongoing investigation and I haven't crossed your clients' names off my suspect list yet."

"No," I said. "You don't."

* * *

It was close to noon and I was meeting a client at Scalo's for lunch. I left the office in Anna's hands and drove across Central. Scalo's is one of the few places in Albuquerque you can approximate a power lunch. I knew that because I counted four guys and one woman talking on their cell phones. My lunch with Janet Balboa wasn't exactly a power move, but it did get her a little closer to her upcoming divorce.

As I passed the university on my way back to the office I made a quick right-hand turn at Yale and went to see Eric Barker. I found him sitting in his office staring at his computer screen, surrounded by piles of papers and empty coffee mugs. He could have used a backhoe himself. Papers spilled off his desk and overflowed the file cabinets, but a space had been cleared for Joni's photograph. She wore a yellow firefighter shirt, a green hard hat, and a radiant smile. She was Eric's beloved daughter; it was killing him that she was gone.

"Eric?" I said.

When he looked up his eyes were returning from a faraway place.

"Are you all right?" I asked him.

He shook his head to clear it. "Neil," he said. "I didn't hear you coming."

"I happened to be in the neighborhood and decided to stop in."

"I'm glad you did. How are you doing? Is the cough any better?"

"Somewhat."

"Here, sit down." He cleared a space for me on a chair. "Can I get you a cup of coffee?"

"No thanks."

"Mind if I have one?"

"Go ahead. I went back to Thunder Mountain last weekend."

"It's hard to go back to the scene of a fire you've been involved in, isn't it?"

Hard, but sometimes necessary. "Yeah. I looked at the house that burned. There was nothing left but ashes and an enormous stone fireplace. I talked to the owner. His girlfriend was distraught, but he didn't seem terribly upset. If you ask me he was seeing dollar signs in the ashes; he had good insurance. Sheila McGraw is checking him out. I also ran into some birders there and they told me they had seen a brown truck with Colorado plates traveling down the road at a high rate of speed that afternoon. They also mentioned that they saw Nancy sitting under the cottonwood tree but they didn't see the backpack."

Eric watched the screen saver moving across his computer screen and said nothing.

"You're sure you didn't see any vehicles that afternoon?" I asked him.

"I'm sure."

"Do you know anybody who has a brown truck with Colorado plates? Another firefighter? An acquaintance of Mike's or Ramona's or Joni's?"

"I can't think of anyone."

"Are you and Nancy members of Forest Sentinels?"

"No."

"I talked to Sheila McGraw this morning. She still believes the fire was set by a professional and she's not willing to rule you and Nancy out yet."

"Nancy's not a professional," he said.

"No, but she did have a firefighter husband and daughter. She's spent a lot of time around firefighters."

"She never took that much interest in it. Fire fighting was an interest Joni and I shared." An interest, I thought, that might have made Nancy feel excluded. "Nancy has always been more interested in quilting and gardening than she is in fighting fires."

"Sheila said Nancy was known to have a hot temper. Where would she have gotten that information from?"

Eric stared at me for a long minute. "Nancy was home alone when they sent the messenger to tell us Joni had died. She went berserk. She screamed and smashed things and hit the guy. I suppose that's what Sheila was talking about."

Some people crumple under disaster, some get angry. I'd already known that anger was Nancy's response. "How did she feel about it afterward?"

"She says she doesn't remember." This raised the question of what else she'd been able to forget.

"I tracked down Ramona and she came back to town and talked to Sheila."

"Good. She needed to do that."

"Sheila says Ramona didn't tell her much. Only that she had left her tribute to Joni and was on her way down the mountain when she saw the fire, heard me screaming, and covered me with her fire shelter."

"If Ramona said that, it's true. She and Joni were very good friends."

"They had a friend named Jackie who lives near Oro? Ramona was staying there before she came back to Albuquerque."

"Jackie?" Eric asked. "I can't think of any friend of Joni's named Jackie." He hit the mouse, chased away the screen saver, and looked at the time in the corner of the screen. "I have to get going soon, Neil. I have a class to teach. Anything else we need to talk about?"

"Not at the moment."

"Well, actually, there is one more thing." His eyes were heading toward his window that looked down on a parking lot.

"What's that?"

"Nancy and I came to an agreement. We've decided to go ahead with the negligence suit as soon as the arson investigation is over."

An agreement, I wondered, or a deal? "What changed your mind?" I asked.

"We're a couple," he said. He stood up. "Thanks for stopping by."

"Glad to do it," I said.

When I got back to the office I called Mike Marshall. Music blared in the background that—to me anyway—sounded less like a hard workout than hard rock. "How you doin', Neil?" he asked.

"Getting better," I said. "I went back to Thunder

Mountain last weekend and came across a couple of things I'd like to talk to you about."

"I'm coming downtown this afternoon. You want me to stop by?"

"Yes," I said.

20

It took about two minutes for Mike Marshall to turn my medium-sized office into a small cell. He was wearing shorts and hiking boots. He seemed bigger and more tightly wound here than he had in the other places we'd met. If he did become an engineer, I hoped he'd have a chance to get out in the field; he'd find an office like Eric Barker's or mine far too confining. But unlike Joni, Mike wouldn't stay twenty-something forever and he wouldn't always be a hotshot. Someday he'd burst through the bubble of his grief. Someday he'd get older, someday he'd slow down. But at the moment I was sitting in front of a guy who was at the peak of his physical power and impatient with being confined to a chair in a lawyer's office.

"So what was it you found at Thunder Mountain?" he asked me.

"A couple of birders told me they saw a brown truck with Colorado plates speeding down the road around the time the fire started. Do you know anybody with a truck that fits that description?" Mike had the kind of mind that would remember make, model, year, speed, license plate number, and color.

He thought about it for a minute and said, "No."

"What kind of car does Ramona drive?" Although I'd met Ramona for lunch I hadn't seen her vehicle. At the time it hadn't seemed important.

"A white Ford pickup with New Mexico plates. I told you she drove up with me that day, didn't I?" This line of questioning wasn't increasing his enthusiasm for being in a lawyer's office.

"Yeah," I said.

He leaned forward in his chair, resting his forearms on his thighs. "What about the guy whose house burned? What kind of vehicle does he drive?"

"A Blazer and a Ferrari."

He leaned back. "That figures."

"Sheila McGraw is investigating, but she still believes the fire was started by a professional."

"There are plenty of them around."

"But only three were known to be on the mountain that day. If it wasn't one of you—"

"It wasn't."

"Then who do you think it could have been?"

He shrugged. "I don't know."

"This friend that Ramona was staying with—does she live in Cloud full-time? Is her vehicle registered in Colorado? Is she a hotshot?"

"You mean Jackie?"

"Yeah."

"Jackie's a guy. His full name is Jake Sorrell. He's the crew boss who hired Joni and Ramona. He was a buddy of theirs, and they always called him Jackie. It was sort of a joke. I don't know what kind of vehicle he drives, but he does live in Cloud full-time. He has a cabin up there. He was injured in the Lone Ridge fire and got government disability. He can afford to live in the woods."

"Lone Ridge is the fire where three firefighters were killed?"

"That's the one." Mike was looking around for the clock that wasn't on my wall, but, sensing warm cinders under the cool ashes of the Lone Ridge fire, I wasn't ready to let him go yet. "Is there Gambel oak in Lone Ridge?"

"Yeah."

"This is the man who prepared the report the government never used?"

"Right. It was a first-class report and he helped prepare a training video, too. If the government had used them Joni and all the hotshots would be alive today, but they just took all that work, knowledge, and experience and put it on the shelf. And look what happened." His voice was bitter.

"Did Sorrell quit because he'd lost crew members at Lone Ridge or because he'd lost the heart for fire fighting?"

"Both, but his injuries would have made it impossible for him to continue even if he'd wanted to. Joni felt she owed him her job, but after a while even she stopped seeing him. It was too depressing. I was never as close to him as Joni and Ramona were."

"What made you think Ramona was at his place?"

"I knew she wasn't at home. You told me she wasn't at her mother's. She didn't have her car and he's the only person I know of that she knows in southern Colorado. I figured Jake heard the news reports about the fire, went into Oro, and picked Ramona up at the hospital. I've never been to his cabin, but Joni told me how isolated it was. It would be a good place to hide out." He stretched out his legs and crossed one foot over the other.

"What does Sorrell look like?"

"Medium-sized, black hair." It wasn't much of a description, but maybe Mike was better at numbers than he was at faces.

"Is his hair long or short?"

"Short when I knew him."

"Is he skinny?"

"No. He had a build like mine, but I haven't seen the guy in a couple of years. What do I know?"

"Is he involved with Forest Sentinels?"

"He could be now. He wasn't when I knew him. Why do you ask?"

"I met someone who was connected to Forest Sentinels when I was in Oro who was very curious about what I was doing. It might be him. I still have the photos Ramona gave me. Would you mind taking a look to see if Jake's picture is in there?"

Mike's feet were itching to hit the trail, but he agreed to look at the pictures.

The bag with the photos and the boots was under my desk. I pulled it out and handed him the manila envelope.

He opened it and began thumbing through the photographs, stopping whenever he came to a painful reminder of Joni.

"Here he is," he said, handing me one of the photos.

It was a group of hotshots in full fire-fighting regalia standing under a tree. I recognized Mike, Joni, and Ramona. None of the guys leaped out of the picture as being the man I'd talked to in McDonald's and none of the women looked like the woman I'd met at Forest Sentinels.

Mike pointed Jake out. "Is that the guy you talked to?"

"I don't know," I admitted. The hotshot he indicated had an orange chain saw slung over his shoulder. He was considerably heavier and stronger than the man I'd met. His smile was wider and his hair was hidden by the hard hat. But he did have dark eyes and a nose that could have been a beak on a thinner face. Take away thirty pounds, turn him into a shadow of what he'd been, and it was possible. The photo was a moment trapped in time. They were all so young and strong and good-looking. Mentally I began turning the hotshots thinner or fatter, grayer and weaker, making the changes that happen slowly over time or rapidly under fire. I had plenty of opportunity to study this photo because Mike had become lost in the one he held. His eyes were tearing, his hands trembling.

"Mike?" I asked. "Are you all right?"

He pressed his fist against his forehead and handed the photos back to me. "Joni was so beautiful," he whispered. "So goddamn beautiful."

"She was." I took a long time putting the photographs under my desk, giving him a chance to regroup. Then I turned the conversation back to Ramona. "Ramona needs help. Hiding out didn't do her any good with Sheila McGraw."

Mike pulled himself out of his fog and became the competent firefighter once again. "What would you have done if you were her?"

"I'd have come back and defended myself." The Hamel way was to dive in and get it over with.

"Yeah, well, you're not Ramona. She knows what to expect from the Forest Service. If you've got a quota to fill, Indians and women are the first people hired. But they're also the first people blamed when anything goes wrong. There's still a lot of resistance to women in the Forest Service."

"The arson investigator is a woman."

"Her boss isn't and her boss's boss isn't either. There are plenty of guys left in the Forest Service who believe women can't hang. The arson investigators are going through the motions of investigating me and Eric Barker. They have to. But we're their own and they don't want to find us guilty. My guess is that if they charge anybody, it'll be Ramona."

"You've talked to Sheila McGraw?"

"Yeah."

"Did you tell her about the disagreement with Hogue?"

"I told her we argued, but I didn't tell her Hogue threatened to fire Ramona. Ramona's got enough strikes against her in the Forest Service without that. A brown person is always a magnet for suspicion in a white person's world."

"Ramona could get herself a lawyer."

"She can't afford to pay a lawyer. So what would she get? A public defender?"

"There are public defenders who do good work."

"Maybe, but the brains in your profession go for the real bucks, don't they?" He had a good attitude toward Indians and women firefighters, but the usual contempt for lawyers.

We've got Indians and women, too, I thought. But what I said was "Not always."

I looked around (ostentatiously, I thought) at the lack of trappings in my office, but he didn't notice.

"I loved Joni. I worked with Ramona. I have a lot of respect for both of them. If Ramona wants to handle this herself, that's her decision."

"Is she still in town?"

"Far as I know she's home with her daughter. Officially, she's on leave from the Forest Service."

"What brought you downtown?" I asked.

"The gas bill was overdue and I had to go to the PNM office to pay it. Is that it?" He was like a kid with feet dangling from the chair pleading to be allowed to leave.

"That's it. Are you going home after you pay the bill?" I hoped he wasn't headed for Ramona's. I wanted to talk to her before he did, but if he knew that, Ramona's trailer could well be his first stop.

"No. I'm going to hike the La Luz Trail." This was a precipitous climb to Sandia Peak full of switchbacks and drop-offs. There were places where you could look down and see the backs of hawks soaring below you. Most people arrived at the top panting, sweating, and out of breath after an all-day climb. Mike could probably make it up and back by nightfall.

"Good idea," I said.

"Let me know if anything new comes up."

"I will."

Mike wasn't a guy who'd get by Anna's desk unnoticed. While we'd been talking she'd been spraying, puffing her hair out a few more inches, and filling the bathroom with noxious fumes. It was a type of mating ritual, but like a peacock flashing its feathers at a quail, it was wasted on Mike. It would take a woman with soot on her face and a hard hat on her head to turn him on. But he did smile at Anna as he left, which made her day.

"Who was *that?*" she asked the minute he was out the door and, I hoped, on his way to climbing Sandia Peak.

"Mike Marshall."

"Is he single?"

"Single, but in mourning. He was Joni Barker's boyfriend."

"The woman with the snakes?"

"That's right."

"It won't be long before somebody snaps him up."

"It'll take a certain kind of woman."

"I guess." She sighed. Anna might like to get to know Mike Marshall better, but I didn't think she'd be willing to pick up snakes and put out fires to do it.

21

I went back into my office and called Sheila McGraw
again. "Anything new on the investigation?" I asked.

"Henry discovered that Ken Roland has a good alibi.
He was in bed with a waitress in Oro."

"Not Karen?"

"No. Somebody else."

"He likes waitresses, doesn't he?"

"Waitresses have time to mess around in the afternoon.
I don't, do you?"

"Not often," I said. "Tell me why you think being in
bed is a good alibi."

"The woman involved claims she'll swear to it in
court."

"Could be he gave her a big tip."

"Could be. But Henry found a witness to corroborate
Ken Roland's story, the property manager of the complex
where the lady friend lives. He saw Roland's Ferrari pull

in that afternoon and it was still there when the guy went off duty at six. A Ferrari isn't the kind of car you're likely to forget."

And no one's likely to forget a large tip. "Thanks for the info," I said.

"I owed you one. You saved me the effort of tracking down Ramona."

"There's always the possibility that somebody else wanted to torch Roland's house, isn't there? Somebody who hated development. One waitress too many, maybe, who bore him a grudge."

"That would make more sense if his lady friends were firefighters."

"They're not his type."

"Too powerful," Sheila agreed.

We said our good-byes and hung up. Then I dialed the number I had for Jackie in Cloud. I got a recorded message saying in singsong operator voice, "We're sorry. You have reached a number that has been disconnected or is no longer in service." I dialed information, asked for a listing for Jake Sorrell, and was told that number had been disconnected.

"Was it 970-555-1240 before it was disconnected?" I asked.

"I can't reveal that information," the operator said. "It was an unlisted number."

The next step was to call Forest Sentinels to establish whether Jake Sorrell was a member. I didn't want to do it myself since the sound of my voice could get the wrong reaction from wolf woman. I asked Anna to make the call.

"Okay," she agreed. "But who's Jake Sorrell?"

"That's what I'm trying to find out."

She dialed the number, fluffing her mane while she waited for someone to answer. "Hi," she said eventually. "Could I talk to Jake Sorrell?"

The question at the other end must have been "Who's calling?" because Anna's answer was "A friend."

"Do you know where I could reach him?" she asked. There was a pause, then she said, "Okay, thanks," and hung up.

"That was a tough lady," she said.

"If it was who I think it was, she keeps a wolf for a pet."

"That figures."

"What did she say?"

"She said he wasn't there and she didn't know where he was."

"Did it sound like she was covering for him?"

"Kinda."

It appeared that Jake had gone even deeper into hiding, and if anybody knew why, it would be Ramona Franklin. I hoped Mike had kept his word and headed for the La Luz Trail, but just in case, I didn't waste any more time getting to Ramona's.

"I'm outta here," I told Anna.

"What should I say if anyone calls?"

"I'm gone for the day."

Guided by landmarks and street numbers I reached

Ramona's trailer in fifteen minutes. Her yard was bare. The guy next door was tending his flowers. Parked in front of the trailer was the white Ford pickup with New Mexico plates that Mike had described, except that he hadn't mentioned it was splattered with mud. The business cards Henry and I left had been taken from the door frame or rattled loose by a power stereo pounding down the street. The doorbell chimed when I pushed it. A little girl wearing a pink flowered dress came to the door. Her black hair was cut in bangs that framed her enormous eyes.

"Hi," she said.

"Hi," I responded.

"My name is Hanna."

"My name is Neil."

"Can you spell Hanna?"

"H-a-n-n . . . a?"

"That's right."

"Can you spell Neil?"

"No." She laughed. "You want to see my mom?"

"Yup."

"Hey, Mom," she yelled.

"I'm coming, Hanna," Ramona replied in her soft, steady voice. She came to the door wiping flour from her hands onto her jeans. "Hi," she said to me. "We're making fry bread." I might have surprised her or Mike might have warned her; her face showed no sign of either. "Come in."

I followed her into the trailer, which was spare and tidy and smelled like something delicious was baking. A small

196

gray, black, and white Navajo rug was tacked to the wall. Textbooks were on the bookshelves. The TV was on but nobody was paying any attention. It was background light and music.

"Do you mind if I finish?" Ramona asked, leading me into the kitchen.

"No, go ahead."

"Hanna always likes this part." Ramona picked up a lump of dough from the kitchen table, rolled it flat, and slipped it into a pan of hot fat on the gas stove. The fat popped and hissed. Hanna laughed and clapped her hands. A drop of fat flew out of the pan and landed in the flame, which blew up in long, hot fingers. If it had been my kitchen I'd have been looking for the fire extinguisher, but Ramona grabbed Hanna, sat down, and waited for the flame to subside. The soot marking the ceiling indicated they'd seen this kind of action before. When Ramona judged the fry bread to be done she took it out to drain and turned off the burner.

"Would you like some?" she asked. "It's good when it's warm."

"Okay," I said. It seemed rude not to accept. Besides, I like fry bread. It seemed even ruder to accept the bread and continue my investigation, but that was something I couldn't help. My life had been saved on Thunder Mountain, but it had been endangered, too. If Ramona was covering for Jake, or if she'd been involved with him, I needed to know.

"Hanna likes it with cinnamon and sugar," Ramona said, sprinkling some powder on Hanna's.

"I'll have mine plain," I said.

Hanna curled up in her mother's lap and licked the sweet stuff from her fingers. Ramona popped the tab from a Miller Lite. "Like a beer?" she asked.

"No thanks," I said. Hanna smiled at me from her mother's arms. I hated to disturb the harmony in the kitchen, but sometimes harmony—like broken bones that haven't been set right—has to be shattered before it can be mended properly. "I went back to Thunder Mountain Sunday," I began. "I ran into some bird watchers and they told me they saw a brown truck with Colorado plates coming down the road at a high rate of speed around the time the fire started. Did you see it?"

Ramona looked down, shook her head, and rested her cheek against Hanna's silky hair.

"Mike told me the Jackie you were staying with in Cloud is Jake Sorrell."

She nodded.

"He also told me Sorrell is the crew boss who hired you and Joni."

"That's right. He did."

"Mike said Jake's very bitter about what happened at Lone Ridge."

"He lost three of his crew there," Ramona said. "That hurt him very much."

"What kind of vehicle does he drive?"

Hanna nestled against her mother, sucked her thumb, and watched me with big, dark eyes. "I don't remember," Ramona said.

"Tom Hogue died on Thunder Mountain," I said, "and

I almost lost my life. If that was Jake's truck and he was there, I need to know."

Ramona hugged Hanna and said nothing.

"What does he look like?" I asked.

"He's kind of skinny."

"Does he have shoulder-length black hair?"

"How did you know?"

"I talked to a man when I was in Oro who must be him. Is he involved with Forest Sentinels?"

"He knows Ellie O'Connor and some other people there."

"I tried to call him, but his phone's been disconnected," I said.

"I didn't know that." Ramona looked up quickly and I glimpsed her eyes. They were black wings beating against the bars of a cage.

"Sooner or later he's going to be questioned," I said. "He's a former firefighter who bears a grudge against the Forest Service and has a connection to a radical environmental organization." If Sheila didn't come across Jake Sorrell herself, I had good reason to turn her on to him. But I thought it would be better if I talked to him first. Somehow I had the idea that if I knew what had happened at Thunder Mountain I could help Ramona better than she'd been helping herself.

"It was my life on that mountain," I continued. "It's my clients who are being treated as suspects." If she chose to, Ramona might have reminded me that I wouldn't be here talking, that I wouldn't have a life, if it hadn't been for her, but she didn't. She asked Hanna if she wanted any more fry bread.

Hanna pouted and said, "No." She was getting the vibe that I hadn't come there just to eat the bread and chitchat.

If I'd asked Ramona what I owed her for saving my life, she would have answered, "Nothing." But in my mind I owed her everything. If nothing else, I could prevent her from taking the rap for a fire Jake Sorrell had planned or started. When it came to motive, Sorrell could beat any of the other suspects. His life had been ruined by fire and the policies of the Forest Service, and it appeared that his vehicle had been on the scene. If Ramona was covering for him, or involved with him, I intended to find out. It might make it darker for Hanna today but a whole lot brighter down the road.

"If you're protecting him, Ramona, you shouldn't be. You have your own life and you have your daughter to think of." Ramona made no response. "Can you tell me how to get to his house?" I asked.

"It would be better if you didn't go."

"I need to talk to him."

"I'll do it." Ramona sighed.

"When?"

"Tomorrow. I can leave Hanna with my aunt and go up there in the morning."

"Maybe you shouldn't go alone." To me Jake was a guy who was very close to the edge. Who knew what would happen if he went over? "He could be dangerous. I can go with you."

"It's okay. Jake is my friend."

We'd finished our fry bread and the time had come for me to leave. "Thanks for the fry bread," I said.

"It's nothing," Ramona replied.

Hanna walked me to the door. The big eyes that had welcomed me when I came in were doing their best to avoid me on my way out.

22

On my way home I thought about Tom Hogue clicking his remote, raising and lowering his hearing level. An amplifier could be a useful device. A hearing-aid store would sell the one Hogue wore, but I thought I was more likely to find what I wanted in I Spy, a store on Menaul that sells surveillance equipment, stun guns, pepper spray, and all the self-defense paraphernalia that's on the fringe of paranoia and legality. I Spy was in a strip mall. No attempt had been made to paint and shape the burglar bars to pretend they were decoration. I Spy was a hard-core, hard-edged, functional kind of place. One of those places where a woman is suspect, even a hard-edged, functional woman.

The guy behind the counter had hair clipped close to his skull and rifle-scope eyes.

"I want something that can pick up a conversation from a distance," I said.

* * *

I stopped at the Kid's shop to try my eavesdropping device out. Los Lobos was blaring and he didn't hear me pull into the parking lot. He was working on a Dodge truck up on the lift and he didn't notice me walk by the open doorway. Mimo did and squawked "Hello," but the Kid didn't pay any attention. "Hello" was one of the few words Mimo knew and he (or she) repeated it often. I walked past the shop and across the field behind it, measuring my paces, casting a long-legged shadow that reached halfway across the field and turned my strides into giant steps. I thought fifty yards would be far enough for my purposes, but I reached the ditch before I got that far. The water was a steady brown flow. The ditches that bring irrigation water into the valley wash garbage and sometimes even bodies out. A plastic container bobbed in the brown stream. Weeds grew tall on the banks. Sunflowers were blooming and dancing in the wind.

I pointed my listening device at the Kid's shop, plugged in the earphones, and clicked it on. First I heard Los Lobos singing "Volver" in the style I call *ranchera grande*, but I didn't consider hearing that a major eavesdropping event. Los Lobos could be heard all over the valley. I fiddled with the controls, turned up the volume, then heard Mimo squawk "Hello" again, which was an accomplishment. Mimo couldn't be heard without help from where I stood. Then the Kid said, "'Adios,' Mimo, say 'adios.'"

"Hello," repeated the bird. The Kid was trying to expand the parrot's vocabulary, possibly even make it bilingual, but Mimo was stubborn. "Hello," it squawked again.

"*Pendejo,*" swore the Kid.

"*Pendejo,*" swore the bird.

I turned the listening device off, crossed the field, and walked into the shop.

"*Hola,* Chiquita," he said. "*Qué tal?*"

"Okay," I said. "And you?"

"Good," he replied.

"You taught Mimo how to swear?"

He was startled. "How did you know that?"

"I could hear you talking from the ditch."

"How could you hear that from all the way back there?"

"*Pendejo,*" the bird cackled again.

"*Cállate,*" said the Kid. Be quiet.

"I bought this listening device on my way home. I was trying it out." Like many people who work with tools, the Kid is fascinated by them in all shapes and sizes. He took the listening device from me and studied it.

"What do you need this for?" he asked.

"It's a long story."

"*Dígame.*"

"Ramóna is going back to Colorado tomorrow to see Jake Sorrell. I think he's the guy I talked to in Oro."

"The guy in McDonald's?"

"Right. If he is Jake Sorrell, he's the crew boss who hired her and she stayed at his place after the fire. I want to hear what they have to say to each other."

"Why?"

"I think he may have started the fire I was in. He was wounded on another fire in Lone Ridge, Colorado, and three of his crew members died. He'd made recommendations that could have prevented the South Canyon disaster, but the Forest Service never listened to him. The truck that was seen near the fire is probably his."

"Ramona was on the mountain then, too, right?"

"Right."

"Do you think they were working together?"

"I don't know, but I intend to find out."

"Why? It's her business, no?"

"No. Sooner or later the arson investigators are bound to get to Jake Sorrell. Suppose he implicates Ramona then? If she won't help herself she needs somebody to help her. I owe her that; she saved my life."

Mimo, whose bright eyes had been bouncing back and forth from me to the Kid, screamed *"Pendejo"* again.

"Quiet, Mimo," I said.

"Why not let the investigator talk to this guy Jake? Why do you have to do it?" I had considered asking the Kid to come with me, but was rapidly changing my mind.

"I don't know if I am going to talk to him," I said. "Maybe I'll just observe."

"You never just observe. And if you find out he started the fire, what do you do then?"

"Try to get him to turn himself in, and if that doesn't work, pass whatever I find on to the arson investigator."

"And if Ramona was involved?"

"I'll see she gets a good lawyer." Jeremy Toner was a public defender I knew who had brains, compassion, and a minimal interest in bucks. I'd have taken Ramona on for nothing myself if that had been possible.

"I don't think you should go," the Kid said.

No shit, I thought, but what I said was "Why not?"

"It's not your business."

"Well, I'm making it my business."

"I didn't like that guy Jake's looks."

Let a man put his clothes in your closet and before you know it he starts telling you who you can hang out with and where you can go.

The Kid turned back to the Dodge pickup, a truck that had seen a lot of hard driving, about two hundred thousand miles worth. "When this guy had his oil changed, somebody put in dirty brake fluid and it polluted the whole system. He was driving when the brakes came on and he couldn't release them. He was lucky. It could have been the other way. He could have stepped on the brakes and have nothing happen." He shook his head. "That would have been a disaster." Was he saying that disastrous accidents happen often enough without looking for them? "It's a big job. The system has to be cleaned out. I promised him I would finish tomorrow. When are you leaving for Colorado?"

"Very early in the morning. I want to get there before Ramona does." He had a clock on his wall and it read eight-thirty. "I ought to go home and go to bed."

"Okay. I stay here till I finish. Maybe I go to my place so you can get up early."

I tried to remember the last night he'd spent at his place, but I couldn't. "All right," I said.

"*Pendejo,*" Mimo screamed, cackling at its little joke.

"Can't you teach that parrot another word?" I asked.

"I'm trying," the Kid said. "Adios?" he offered, but the parrot didn't bite. It liked the reaction it had been getting to *pendejo*.

The Kid went back to work on the Dodge's polluted system. I went home and looked up Cloud on the map. It was a small town about fifteen miles south of Thunder Mountain as the bird (or helicopter) flies, and about ten miles from Oro. It was at the edge of the National Forest, quiet enough and close enough that a helicopter flying overhead wouldn't go unnoticed. I got into bed and made an offering to the sleep god that the god did not accept. I chased dreams around my bed for a few hours, then went outside to watch the moon, which was turning the field behind my house into a rippling estuary with a white horse running through the waves. I looked through the V between the trees and the horse came up and let me rub its nose.

"What do you think? Should I go to Cloud?" I asked. The horse neighed and ran away.

I went back inside and slept until the moon came round the bedroom wall of the house and beamed in the window. Then I got up, walked down the hall to the empty room, opened the door, and went in. I looked in the closet and saw nothing but a charred and crinkly reminder of death. A tree branch scratched at the skylight. The moon shone in, turning the room the color of ghosts. I couldn't exactly see them, but I knew they were there: the ghosts of the family that had once farmed this property, the ghost of Joni Barker, the ghost of Tom Hogue, Joe's ghost. One day mine would be hanging out here, too, unless the place got torn down or had occupants that were too busy to notice. The dead have their own language. One message they send is to look out for the living.

Even in a roomful of ghosts, Joe's stood out. "Why are you going?" it asked.

"I do this kind of stuff because you didn't," I replied.

"That doesn't mean you have to pursue every suspect and face down every challenge," the ghost replied.

"When you choose a path you have to follow that path until it ends, don't you?"

"Sometimes the path forks and you can take a different direction," the ghost said.

"I haven't reached that point yet."

"Then go for it," said the ghost.

There was no use trying to sleep after that, so I loaded my thirty-eight, put my listening device in my backpack, got in the Nissan, and let the moon guide me to Colorado.

23

Since a gun in a glove compartment or a backpack is a concealed weapon and illegal in New Mexico, I put the thirty-eight on the floor. There were few cars on the highway; I went at my own speed. No trucks to pass, no motorcycles to pass me, no junkers without turn signals to get in the way. I settled into the rhythm of the road and the four hours went by like a trip to the grocery. The sun was rising as I got to Cloud. A misty film filled the valley. On top of that was a green layer of trees, then dark, hulking mountains and an orange sky shading to a pale green glow. A red *K* inside a red circle lit a convenience store with a surreal light. I pulled in for doughnuts and coffee. The coffee was brewed and black, although it had the taste of instant from the tap. The doughnut I picked had a dark chocolate glaze. The lone clerk seemed relieved that the night shift was just about over and I didn't look like a person who'd be packing a piece.

There was a risk involved in the question I was about to ask. The phone on the counter could be used to call the person I was inquiring about, but most likely the answer would be a message about the line being disconnected. And I wasn't going to locate Jake Sorrell without asking somebody.

"I'm looking for a guy named Jake Sorrell," I said. "Do you know where he lives?"

The clerk took my money and counted out the change. "Don't know him," the clerk answered. "I'm new in town."

I went outside, sat on a milk crate, ate my doughnut, drank my coffee. The morning was cool enough that I could see steam rising from the Styrofoam cup. The air had that early morning freshness that'll lead you to believe you can leave your mark on the day. It was damper than I'm used to and it wasn't just the dew. A front was moving in. Clouds already shadowed the horizon. It was the hour when some go off to work and some go out to hunt. Several trucks passed by with rifles balanced like levels across their rear windows. I threw my cup in the trash, got back in the Nissan, and continued searching for Jake Sorrell.

A few miles further down the road I came across another convenience store, a Diamond Shamrock. This time the clerk was a sleepy woman. I got another cup of muddy coffee and asked again about Jake Sorrell.

"Jake." She yawned. "Where does he live? On Sagebrush Ridge, I think. Turn left, go down the road a ways. You'll see the sign."

"Any idea how far 'a ways' is?"

"Couple of miles, I think."

"Thanks," I said.

I drove ten long miles before I came to the Sagebrush Ridge sign. The letters had been carved into the wood and the lots would probably sell for a hundred grand. It didn't strike me as the place Jake Sorrell called home, but I drove around the winding roads anyway, looking for a brown truck. All I saw were trophy four-by-fours and cedar-shake roofs. Maybe the convenience clerk had been confused, maybe she'd been trying to confuse me. In any case the sun was up, time was passing, Ramona would be on the road, and it was important to get to Jake's before she did.

I figured the people at Forest Sentinels would know where Jake lived, but coaxing that information out of wolf woman might require more powers of persuasion than I possessed. Still, I'd run out of convenience stores and Forest Sentinels seemed like my best bet, so I drove into Oro. The office happened to be open and the person sitting at the desk was a man in his twenties wearing khakis and a cotton shirt. Blond bangs flopped across his forehead.

"I'm a friend of Jake Sorrell's," I said. "I thought he lived in Sagebrush Ridge, but I drove all around there and it doesn't look like his kind of place."

"No," the man smiled, "it's not. Jake lives off Sagebrush Trail. It's a very different neck of the woods. Go back to the highway, go north six miles, and you'll see a small sign on the right that says Sagebrush Trail. There'll be a couple of miles of paved road before it turns to dirt.

Keep going and when you get to the big rock, turn left. You can't miss it; Jake's cabin is the only one on the left fork."

"Thanks a lot."

"Glad to help," he said.

Finding Sagebrush Trail with his directions was a piece of cake, although the trip into Oro had wasted precious time. The paved road headed west across a green valley where horses grazed. There were a couple of trailers beside the road, some A-frames, and a log cabin. This was the working-class side of the mountain, a pocket of rural poverty in an area of distant beauty that reminded me of my own neighborhood. I had a big city breathing down my neck. These people had big money. The paved road continued for a couple of miles, then entered the foothills, where it became dirt. This, I figured, would be where the plowing stopped in the winter and the mud started in spring. Anyone who lived beyond here would have to make his own arrangements to get in or out in winter. Whatever color Jake's truck was, it would need a large plow. I drove the dirt road trailing a dust parachute behind me, looking for the large rock and wondering what the difference is between a rock and a boulder. A boulder is a detached entity, I decided. You can have a rock face, but not a boulder face. There were several of either (or both) beside the road and in the field, but no roads that led left.

The flatness of the valley and the road pointing toward the mountains were familiar. It wasn't that I'd been in similar sites in New Mexico, although I had. It was that

I'd seen this valley before—from the air. The Forest Service helicopter flew over here before it descended into South Canyon. Anyone below could have seen the chopper fly over and land, identifying it as belonging to the Forest Service. A helicopter's insistent buzz is hard to ignore. It's an annoying mosquito. It's a traffic reporter covering a Big-I wreck. It's the sound of surveillance. It's the sound of war. The peak in front of me was the top of Thunder Mountain. If I looked carefully I could see the black.

The road began to climb. The grass turned to piñon and juniper. My ears popped. Piñon-juniper became aspen. I didn't meet another car, which was fortunate because the road was only wide enough for one. This road got so little traffic it hardly even had ruts. My thirty-eight was on the floor, but being out here in the woods made me wish I had a rifle across my rear window. While I was wondering if my thirty-eight could shoot as far as the listening device could hear, the road took a sudden dip. I came up the other side and faced a rock the size of a wall. One fork of the road went to the left of the rock, the other bore right. The left fork had been defaced by hand-painted signs that read "Keep Out," "No Trespassing," and "Not Responsible for Accidents on Private Property." That sign had been pockmarked by bullets. The road on the right said nothing. I took it, looking for somewhere to leave the Nissan.

When I found a place I could pull off I parked, closing the door quietly and locking it. I put the thirty-eight in my backpack and began walking through the woods looking for the "Keep Out" road, listening to the sound of a gurgling stream. When you're lost in the woods the best way out is to find water and follow the flow. I wasn't lost yet, but I'm always drawn to the sound of running water. There are times in New Mexico when I miss water—I'll admit it—but there were times in the East when I thought I'd die without sun. I reached the stream at a place where it could be crossed easily by stepping on stones. When I got to the other side I followed the water until it lapped up against the back side of the rock and formed a pool. The sun was still a couple of steps ahead of the clouds and it turned the water the color of Jack Daniel's. Light reflected from the surface of the pool and flickered across the rock, making it appear to be on fire. I dropped a stone into the pool and watched the rippling circles spread. But the reflections on the rock's surface were less predictable. They boiled and churned and curled in and out of the rough spots like smoke until a cloud covered the sun and put the light show out.

The stream split at the rock. I took the north fork, followed it to a culvert that went under the "Keep Out" road, and continued on the road, staying close to the edge of the forest in case I heard someone coming and needed to duck for cover. I heard nothing but leaves rustling, squirrels chattering, and my footsteps crunching the dirt. The clouds and the sun were doing a little dance, lending me a shadow and taking it away again. I'd walked for about a mile when I saw the sun, which had escaped temporarily from the clouds, beaming into a clearing ahead. I entered the woods and circled around the clearing, keeping trees between me and the open space. When I reached a spot where the undergrowth was thick, I got down on my knees and crawled through the brush until I could see into the clearing. I saw a cabin made out of boards that had weathered old-barn gray. The windows had small panes with the opacity of one-way glass. The cabin had a metal chimney, a steep tin roof that the snow would slide off, and a woodpile that was several cords thick. There was a garden with cornstalks tall enough to hide a marijuana patch and staked tomato plants the size of a man. I was looking at subsistence living, maybe even survivalist living. It was the kind of place the FBI likes to stake out and shoot up. Inside an open shed a chain saw, a bunch of tools, and a plow were visible. Parked behind the house was a relatively new brown Ford truck with Colorado plates and a rifle leveled across the rear window of the cab.

I aimed my eavesdropping device at the cabin, turned it on, plugged in the earphones, and heard nothing but the leaves rustling in the trees—which I'd been hearing without the device. Hoping the batteries hadn't gone dead, I gave it a shake, turned it off, then on again, listened, and heard the distant but distinct sound of a cough and a man's voice swearing. Someone was in the house and someone had coughed, reminding me that I hadn't had a Ricola since I'd left the car. I unwrapped one and popped it in my mouth, turned the device off to save the batteries, then lay down on my stomach and settled in to wait. I'd left earlier than intended, but it had taken longer than I expected to find Jake's cabin.

Waiting isn't my forte. I can do it when I have to, but this wasn't a very comfortable wait. The clouds had taken possession of the sun and the air had the damp, charged feeling that precedes a hard rain. A fly buzzed in and out of my hair and ants crawled up my legs. I rested my head on my arm and snuggled into the ground, trying not to cough or scratch. My arm went numb, but there was no way to shake some feeling back into it without standing up and blowing my cover. I couldn't see any sign of Jake, but that didn't mean he wasn't inside looking out through the panes of one-way glass.

It wasn't long before wheels came barreling down the road. Ramona's, I hoped. The vehicle I saw through the underbrush was her white truck and she was alone in it. She stepped out, slammed the door behind her, and the sound resounded like a rifle volley through the clear mountain air. It couldn't have been often that Jake Sorrell heard a vehicle approach. That would have brought him out if the sound of the slammed door hadn't.

As he stepped from the darkness of the cabin into the light I saw that Jake Sorrell was my man. He walked toward Ramona with a slight limp that I hadn't noticed when we'd met in McDonald's. He and Ramona hugged. He was wearing black, and next to her he looked even frailer than he had earlier.

I turned on my listening device and heard her say, "Hi, Jackie."

"Hey, Ramona."

They stepped apart. Ramona stood in front of him with her arms at her sides, a sturdy, steady figure in her faded jeans.

"How are you?" Jake asked. His gravelly voice crackled though my eavesdropper like static.

"I'm okay." Her voice had its measured softness. "Your garden's looking good."

"It's coming along. How's Hanna?"

"She's good. You don't look well today."

"It's the weather. Whenever there's a front moving in I hurt. Why did you come back? There's trouble?"

Ramona nodded. "Yes."

"What happened?"

"Somebody saw a truck like yours in the drainage the day of the fire."

"Who told you that?" He raised his head and the hair fell away from his thin face.

"The lawyer who is working for the Barkers. She said she talked to you when she was in Oro."

"That's who that woman was? The Barkers' lawyer?"

"Yes. She went back to the East Canyon Sunday and talked to some bird watchers. They're the ones who told her they saw the truck."

"Did they get a license plate number?"

"I don't know."

"They can't trace the truck if they don't have a license number," Jake said.

"The lawyer said that because of what happened at Lone Ridge and because you are connected to Forest Sentinels the arson investigator will be looking for you."

"Forest Sentinels wasn't involved. Nobody will be able to pin anything on them. They don't even know I did it."

"She said that sooner or later the investigators will find out about the truck and they will find you."

"Don't worry." Jake pushed his hair back and smiled slightly. "I can be gone long before they get here."

"Where will you go?"

He shrugged. "Anywhere."

"The arson investigators will keep on looking for you. They know the fire was started by a firefighter. They suspect Mike Marshall. They suspect Eric and Nancy Barker." What she didn't say was that she had been the prime suspect. "We were all on the mountain that day."

Jake looked down at the ground. His voice turned into a mumble that I needed total concentration to pick up. "You gotta believe that I didn't know any of you were there," he said.

"I believe you. I already told you that."

"When I heard the helicopter I thought it was more Forest Service investigators going back to do more studies, to write another report. Did you ever read what they said?"

She shook her head. "No."

"They blamed the hotshots."

"I know."

"If they'd used my report, nobody would have ever died at South Canyon. The Incident Commander never would have sent a crew in there if he'd been educated about Gambel oak. Joni Barker died because the Forest Service put her life and every other firefighter's life at risk. And for what? To save somebody's goddamn house. Joni was murdered as sure as if they'd put a gun to her head. She was one of the best people who ever lived. The Forest Service fucked up and then they blamed the victims. I was out here when the helicopter went overhead. I cracked. I wanted that house to burn. I wanted the Forest Service investigators to suffer the way Joni and the others did."

Ramona looked around the clearing in the woods. "You stayed here too long, Jackie, alone with your grief. That's not the way out. Having Hanna and my family has helped me so much. The man who died in the fire had children. He had people who cared about him."

"What do you think I should do? Turn myself in?"

"It will go better for you if you work with them. The lawyer could find someone to represent you."

"I could disappear." He smiled. "I'm good at that."

"Disappearing won't restore the balance. When there is trouble I go back to the reservation. You could come with me. Talk to the elders."

The wind was picking up and rustling Jake's cornstalks. "I would never have deliberately endangered you or Mike or Nancy and Eric Barker," he said.

"It's all right, Jackie. We know fire. We weren't in danger."

"Does anybody know you're here?"

"Only the lawyer."

"Did you tell her you knew what I had done?"

"I didn't tell anybody. I will never tell anybody." She spoke with a ferocity that convinced me.

"Thanks." He touched her arm. "Let me think and decide what to do."

"All right," she said.

"Can you stay?"

"No. I have to get back to Hanna."

"I'll go into town and call you when I am ready. You want to take some tomatoes back with you?"

"Okay."

Jake went into the garden and came back with an armful of ripe tomatoes. Nothing tastes as good as a tomato fresh from the garden, but neither of them took a bite. Ramona put hers in the truck, got in the driver's seat, and headed back down the road. Jake kept one. He stood still, tossing it from one hand to the other and staring after Ramona. When her truck could no longer be heard tearing up the road, he caught the tomato in his right hand and squeezed it until all the juice, seeds, and pulp ran out. Then he went back in his cabin.

Lightning flashed near Thunder Mountain and I wondered what he'd do next. Being in a fire can damage a person badly. So can seeing your friends die, and so can killing someone. Jake was responsible for one house torched and Tom Hogue's death. He'd known the Forest Service was on the mountain. A good case could be made for premeditation. He might decide to get himself a lawyer, cop a plea, and exonerate Ramona. He might load up his truck, hit the road, and disappear. He might think Ramona was the only one who stood between him and jail. I'd believed her when she said she wouldn't turn him in. It could makes things very difficult for her, except that I had Jake's confession on tape. It was in her and my clients' best interests to get my tape to Sheila McGraw. I put it in my backpack and headed for my car.

24

The thick, damp air settled like a weight upon my shoulders and head. My backpack felt heavier going out than it had coming in, although the contents remained the same. Drops of rain spattered the leaves and pinged the ground. At the moment it was a gentle rain. The Navajos speak of a he-rain and a she-rain. This one felt like a she. I figured I had about a mile to go before I reached the stream that would lead me to my Nissan. I made my way through the woods, mostly aspen, listening to the sound of my footsteps and the sound of the rain until the whooshing, rustling sounds were interrupted by the roar of a vehicle racing down the "Keep Out" road. A door slammed. I hoped it wasn't Ramona coming back. Jake Sorrell had been relatively calm on the outside, but inwardly he had to be a guilt-ridden, desperate man. I stopped and listened, wanting to go forward, wondering if I should go back. After a few minutes the door slammed again and a vehicle sped back down the road.

I continued hiking, one foot in front of the other. An aspen forest isn't as dense as some others. The slender trunks are a silvery color and in the rain the spaces between the trees fill up with shadows and ghosts. I was listening for the smooth sound of the rushing water that would guide me out of the woods when I heard the sharp sound of a twig snap behind me. I spun around, and saw nothing but tree trunks and leaves. I started walking again, but more lightly this time, doing as little as possible to rustle the leaves. I went a few yards further and heard another snap, only this one was louder and closer, a bigger branch, a heavier foot. Even the most dangerous animal you might encounter in the woods—a bear—is only dangerous if you come upon one unexpectedly. Bears don't stalk people. The only animal likely to be stalking me was another human. I thought about taking my thirty-eight out of my pack, but a gun is useless if you can't see what's coming, and I didn't want to give in to paranoia. There was a possibility that Ramona was out there and too much harm can be done by a paranoid with a gun. I called out, "Who's there?" But only the rain answered.

I continued walking, heard the sound of rushing water pick up, and stopped hearing the sound of snapping twigs. Either the stream was drowning out the sound of the stalker or the stalker had been the product of an imagination in overdrive. I followed the stream to the reflecting pool. The rain fell into the pool in steady drops, water blending into water. The clouds had put out the light show and the rock was a flat, dull gray.

I walked along the bank to the spot where I'd crossed

before, hitched up my pack, and stepped onto the stones and into the open. If anyone was going to attack me this seemed like the optimum moment, but no one did. It wasn't much further to my yellow Nissan. I crossed the road, took my keys from my pocket, inserted the key into the lock. Concentrating too hard on what might have been behind me, I'd forgotten to consider what lay ahead. The bushes adjacent to the car rustled and a woman burst out. The rain had turned her gray-blond hair into Medusa curls and it swirled wildly around her head. It was Ellie O'Connor, the woman from Forest Sentinels, and she held a tire iron in her hand. Hers, I figured; there was no sign that my car had been broken into.

The thirty-eight in my backpack could do considerably more damage than her tire iron, but her weapon had the advantage of being in her hand. As I struggled to twist out of my backpack, she smashed the top of the Nissan with her tire iron and the sound of metal hitting metal reverberated through the woods. "When you get out of that backpack, drop it on the ground," she said.

I did as I was told.

"What are you doing here?" she asked me.

"How did you know I was here?" I asked, although I figured I already knew.

"Randall, the guy who works for me, said you'd come to the office looking for directions to Jake's. When I heard that, I drove on up. Jake said he hadn't seen you, but I took a look down this road and found your car."

Why do you care who visits Jake? would have been my next question, but I hadn't answered hers yet. "I'm a lawyer from Albuquerque. I'm representing Eric and Nancy Barker, whose daughter was killed in the South Canyon fire."

"Jake told me that. It doesn't explain why you're here." She began slapping the tire iron against the palm of her hand.

My own hand was itching to be inside my pack. "Ramona Franklin saved my life in the East Canyon fire. She came up here to talk to Jake. If she was in danger I wanted to be here for her."

"Why would talking to Jake put her in danger?"

We were enmeshed in dripping, weeping sounds. Water soothes rough spots, but the answer to that question was a hard truth no matter how you chose to look at it. It's one thing to shout let it burn; it's another to actually strike the match. Ellie must have wondered whether Jake had started the fire. She'd reached the moment when she'd have to find out.

"He's your friend, right?" I asked.

"Yes."

"Then you should ask him."

She stared at my blue backpack lying on the ground as if wishing she had X-ray vision. "What's in the pack?"

"A listening device, a gun."

"Push it over here with your foot."

I followed orders. She cradled the tire iron in the crook of her arm, opened the pack, took out the gun, emptied the bullets onto the ground, opened the listening device, and took out the tape. "You recorded Jake's conversation with Ramona?"

"Yes. My clients are suspects in the fire. That tape could keep them and Ramona out of jail."

"But what will it do for Forest Sentinels?"

"It will eliminate any suspicion that Forest Sentinels started the fire."

"Jake's a member of Forest Sentinels. If he was involved we'll always be suspect. This tape could ruin us."

Jake had said Forest Sentinels wasn't involved. Whether that would be good enough for her or not I didn't know. Forest Sentinels was her baby and her wolf. She had the tape in her hand and she had the power to destroy it. As a witness to Ramona and Jake's conversation I was useless without the tape. I had too many vested interests to be believable. But she didn't know that and she might not believe me if I told her. Several people had known I was coming here. She was the only one who'd known I'd arrived. Her fingers tightened around the tire iron. She stared at the tape with angry eyes, and I had to wonder just how much Forest Sentinels meant to her. "There's a tape deck in my car, why don't you play it?"

"I don't want to hear it," she said.

I thought I knew why. We were still in the murky area of my word against Jake's. She could dismiss my word, but once she heard the tape her conscience might force her to act.

We were so deep in our thoughts neither one of us heard Jake until his boot heel hit the road. A black cowboy hat shielded his face. The rain was falling harder now. It pelted the brim of his hat and drummed on the roof of the car. To me it had the sound of a he-rain. Jake carried a thirty-thirty and his face wore a bitter smile.

"You taped my conversation with Ramona?" he asked.

"That's right."

"What did you intend to do with it?"

"Turn it over to the arson investigators."

"And you, Ellie? What are you going to do with it?"

"Destroy it," she said.

"You don't want to hear what's on it?"

"No, I don't." Her eyes were wide and fierce.

"So that leaves you, me, and Ramona who know, but your word won't mean much in court," he said to me. He was right about that. "Ramona promised she wouldn't tell and I believed her."

So had I.

"And Ellie, you're going to do whatever it takes to protect Forest Sentinels, aren't you? Even if it means shielding me."

"It's my life, Jake. You know that."

"So that leaves me." Jake held up the rifle and stared as if he could see his reflection in the shiny black barrel. "And what are you gonna do, Jackie?" he said. "Blow town and leave some good people high and dry. Is that what you're gonna do?" He snapped the lever, cocked the hammer, and pointed the rifle at Ellie.

"Put the gun down, please," she said.

"Drop the tire iron. Hand over the tape."

She did as she'd been ordered, extending the tape in the palm of her hand. But he left it lying there and turned the rifle toward me. "And you, Ms. Attorney? What do you think I oughta do?"

"Get a good lawyer. Plea-bargain. Cut yourself a deal."

"But any deal I cut's gonna mean jail time, isn't it?"

"Probably."

"You've seen where and how I live. Would you want to go to jail after living like this at the edge of the wilderness?"

I wouldn't want to go to jail after living in an apartment with a view of the Dumpster in the parking lot, but my answer was "If you don't do the time, someone else could be doing it for you. Ramona, maybe, or the Barkers. Is that what you want?"

"No," he said slowly. "That's not what Jackie would want."

He aimed the rifle at Ellie. "Give her back the tape," he ordered.

"Are you crazy, Jake?"

"Give her the tape."

"What about Forest Sentinels?"

"Forest Sentinels will survive. The tape says I acted alone."

"We've been too outspoken. Nobody will believe that."

"They'll believe it because the lawyer here's gonna make sure everybody believes it, aren't you?"

"I'll do my best," I said.

Ellie handed me the tape. I took the keys from my pocket, opened the car door, tossed the tape in, and stuck the keys back in my pocket.

Jake's eyes had been those of a wounded and trapped animal, but he turned the gun toward himself, stared into the black hole of the barrel, and saw the way out.

"Don't, Jake, please. There's another solution," Ellie pleaded.

"I've done too much hard time in my life. I don't want to do any more."

"You'll get out eventually," Ellie said. "You'll be able to start another life."

He placed his finger on the trigger and stared even deeper into the barrel while the rain pelted us with its hard, driving power.

"That's not what Ramona and the people who care about you would want," I said. "Think of them."

He looked up with dark fire in his eyes. "I hurt when it rains. I hurt when it doesn't. I hurt every minute of every day. That was my crew, my buddies on Lone Ridge and Thunder Mountain. I couldn't save them then. I want to be with them now." He looked beyond us as if seeing ghosts in the mist that whispered, "Come." "This is for them."

"Don't!" Ellie screamed.

But Jake Sorrell put the barrel under his chin, pulled the trigger, and blew his head off.

25

A long drive back to Albuquerque was followed by a long night listening to branches scratching at my skylight. The Kid slept beside me, though, and that helped.

Sheila McGraw called in the morning. "Looks like you got our man," she said.

"Not in the way I would have chosen," I replied.

"If he was guilty he was looking at a long sentence. Given the circumstances we could have made a good case for premeditation. Sorrell bore a major grudge against the Forest Service. He must have been aware that Forest Service personnel were on Thunder Mountain. The helicopter flew right over his cabin. Henry Ortega found some local women who'd seen a truck like Sorrell's in the drainage shortly before the fire started. If I'd killed an innocent person and was about to be found out, I might have blown my own head off. There was no suicide note that we were able to find."

"In a way there was."

"Yeah?"

"He spoke to Ramona before he died and I made a tape of their conversation."

"You planning on turning it over?"

"I am," I said, reaching for a Ricola.

"What made you go up there, anyway?" Sheila asked.

"It appeared to me that Ramona was covering for Jake. She told me she was going to his house to talk to him. I figured she might try to convince him to turn himself in. Who knows what his reaction would have been? She wasn't doing anything to protect herself, so I tried to do it for her."

"You could have given us a call."

I could have, but I'd done it my way, the Hamel way.

The question I had to keep asking myself was whether the outcome would have been any better if I had called Sheila with my information instead of passing it on to Ramona and going up to Colorado myself. Jake Sorrell might be rotting in jail instead of lying in the ground. He probably would have tried to exonerate Ramona if they'd caught him, but would anybody have believed him? He might also have killed himself without exonerating Ramona. And then where would she be? Those were questions I could go on asking forever but never be able to answer.

"If you're right and your tape absolves Ramona of any involvement in the East Canyon fire I'll be happy to be done with this incident," Sheila said. "It's been a sorry episode in the history of the Forest Service."

She was right about that. "Will Ramona get her job back?" I asked.

"That'll depend on what the OSHA investigation turns up. There's still the lookout issue. I'll let you know if I hear anything."

"Thanks," I said.

The East Canyon arson investigation was closed. Forest Sentinels was absolved of any involvement. No criminal charges were filed against Ramona, Mike Marshall, or the Barkers, although Ramona remained on suspension from the Forest Service. Both Ramona and Mike went back to school. The Barkers had made their own private arrangement and they wanted to continue with the negligence suit. I advised them to wait, however, until the OSHA report was completed. Sheila McGraw never did call me about it, but in March the report was finished and a copy was delivered to the Barkers. Eric brought it by for me to read and we made an appointment to get together and discuss their options.

I took it home and curled up on the sofa to read it while the Kid worked late at the shop. The last night I could remember him spending at his house was the night before I went back to Colorado. You could say he was living in my place, but with an option. He hadn't given up his rental house yet. The empty room remained empty.

The OSHA report determined that management made willful and serious violations on the South Canyon fire. Training had been inadequate concerning the dangers of fighting a Gambel oak fire even though that information had been made available to the Forest Service. There should have been aerial surveillance. The Forest Service's weather information should have been communicated to the firefighters. The report made recommendations for improving working conditions for both the supervisors and the firefighters, but no criminal charges were filed. Whatever action was taken against management was an internal matter.

I read the section on aerial surveillance carefully. The interagency report had implied negligence on the part of the lookout, but the OSHA report exonerated Ramona. It concluded that the blowup would not have been visible from Ramona's post on the ridge. The report was in many ways a victory for the dead firefighters and their families. It was definitely a victory for Ramona.

I called her as soon as I got to work in the morning. "Have you seen the OSHA report?" I asked.

"I heard about it," she replied with the sound of a smile in her voice.

"It must be very gratifying to you."

"It feels good," she said. "The best part is I get my job back. I've been reinstated."

"That's wonderful" was one response. Mine was "Do you still want to go back on the line after all that's happened?" It was dirty, dangerous work.

"I have to," she replied, and I didn't think she was talking about the money. "The Gathering of Nations Powwow is this weekend and Hanna will be dancing. Would you like to come?"

There are powwows all over the West, but the annual Gathering of Nations held in the Pit, UNM's basketball arena, is the largest and most spectacular of all. People from all over the Americas attend. "I'd love to," I said.

"We'll see you there," Ramona answered.

I hadn't met with the Barkers for several months and I was interested to see how far they'd traveled down the grief road. Nancy looked about the same. She wore jeans and her T-shirt was so neat it might have been pressed. Her lipstick had been carefully applied. Her hair was smooth and in place. The engine was still running but no longer in overdrive. She wasn't wearing the green ribbon over her heart and neither was Eric. Some of the mist around him had parted. He seemed more in focus. His clothes weren't as rumpled and most of the time he was able to keep his eyes within the confines of my office. The view out the window this time of year was nothing but a stripped tree anyway.

"Would you like water or coffee?" I asked.

"Water," Nancy replied.

"Coffee. No sugar," said Eric. "How are *you* doing?" he asked when I came back with the drinks.

"Better. I think I've finally coughed out all the smoke."

"Have you quit smoking?" Nancy asked.

"I'm working on it."

"What do you think of the OSHA report?" Nancy took a sip of her water.

"They did find negligence on the part of the Forest Service."

Nancy finished her water and put the empty glass down on my desk without, I noticed, leaving a trace of lipstick on the rim. "Right, but what are they going to do about it?" It was a rhetorical question. She'd already read the report; she already knew the answer.

But I went ahead and restated it. "They recommended some changes in Forest Service policy. The report indicates no criminal charges will be filed."

"So what do the negligent officials get then? A slap on the wrist?" she asked.

"More or less," I replied. "But OSHA did find negligence and that could help your case enormously. Have you talked to the other families? How do they feel?"

"Vindicated," said Eric.

"You have a much better chance of winning than when we last spoke, but it will still be difficult emotionally." The odds had improved, but the pain was still there. It was an inflated balloon that filled the office. The Barkers had the choice of keeping it pumped up or letting the air run out.

"We know that," said Eric.

"Have you made a decision?" I asked, turning a pencil over and over in my fingers and listening to the fan on my computer hum.

Eric cleared his throat, but Nancy was the one to speak first. "We've decided not to sue," she said.

"We don't need the money," said Eric, "and, as I told you before, suing won't bring our daughter back." His point of view had won. Whatever the determining factor had been, this was only one of a series of intermarital negotiations in a long and deep relationship. "What we really wanted was for the Forest Service to stop blaming the firefighters."

"To accept responsibility for their errors," said Nancy.

"And to take steps to see that this never happens again," said Eric.

"That, too," Nancy agreed.

"I hope you don't think we've wasted your time, Neil." Eric was watching me with his gray eyes.

"No," I said. "I think you made the right decision." But when I looked out my window I saw a bundle of money sprout wings and fly away. I put down my pencil. The lawsuit issue had been resolved, but it wasn't the only issue on my mind. The photographs and the fire-fighter boots were still in the bag beneath my desk. "You know the OSHA report also determined that there should have been aerial surveillance of the South Canyon fire and that the lookout would have been unable to see the blowup from her post. Ramona has been exonerated and reinstated by the Forest Service. She'll be going back on the line next summer."

"Good for her," Eric said.

"The Gathering of Nations Powwow is next weekend and Ramona's daughter is dancing. She asked me to come. I was wondering if you'd like to join us."

This silence was bigger and deeper. For me it would be the final resolution of both fires. Eric looked at Nancy with hope in his eyes. "What do you think, Nan?"

"I'd like that," she said.

"Good," I replied. "I have the boots here that Joni gave

Ramona and some photos of Joni and the hotshots. Do you want them?"

"Yes," Eric said.

"Maybe there'll be some of Joni we haven't seen yet," Nancy said hopefully.

"Maybe so." I handed them the package and we made arrangements to meet at a ticket booth outside the Pit. I walked them to the door and watched them head back to the East Mountains.

"They gonna sue?" Anna asked the minute the door was closed.

"They decided not to," I replied.

"Damn." She shook her mane. "Why not?"

"OSHA found negligence and the Barkers were satisfied with that."

"But the money could be so good!" Anna said. The federal government's pockets went way deep. Anna had looked into them and seen a bigger office and maybe even an assistant, someone to answer the phone while she attended her hair. But I liked the size of my office and was satisfied with the shape of my hair.

"Not *that* good," I replied.

Mike Marshall came to the powwow with the Barkers. The Kid accompanied me and I introduced everybody to each other at the ticket booth. The Kid and Mike were about the same age, but the Kid was taller and skinnier and he looked ten years older. Fire fighting is a tough job; border-crossing is a tough life. Mike's burns had healed and his eyes had the keenness of a quarterback who sees better and farther than everyone else.

We bought our tickets and found seats about halfway down the side of the arena. I figured that Ramona would be busy with her daughter's dance but would find us somehow when she was ready. The Pit has a slope worthy of the black diamond marking an expert ski trail. Nancy ended up with the aisle seat. Eric was beside her, then me, the Kid, and Mike. A circle of men was drumming on the floor with a power that made conversation insignificant. It might have been the amplification; it might have been the acoustics in the Pit. I thought I had never heard such powerful drumming. Some men dressed in cowboy clothes were dancing a slow, shuffling dance. A couple of them looked like white dudes to me, but sometimes it's hard to tell what's white, what's Indian, what's a combination. I'd brought my Aunt Joan's birding binoculars, but even after I glassed the whitest men I still couldn't be sure.

The announcer, a well-known Indian actor, said the grand entry would begin with two thousand dancers. They poured down the stairs and onto the floor wearing feathers, beads, shells, ribbons, skins, furs, silver, and fringe. Red, orange, gold, blue, magenta, and emerald green were a few of the colors. They wore headdresses and moccasins, loincloths and dresses, shawls and capes. Numerous nations were represented from the Arctic Circle to Tierra del Fuego. The color was ecstatic. The activity was intense. Sioux, Crow, Arapaho, Cheyenne, and Navajo were some of the North American tribes who danced down the stairs. The dancers flowed into the floor of the Pit, filled it, and began moving in a circular pattern.

"It looks like thousands of parrots," said the Kid. But the sound was better. Several groups had set their drums up on the floor and were passing the beat around.

The grand entry dance continued for a long time in a swirling circle of rhythm and color. Eventually the dancers filed off the floor and were followed by one of those long pauses common to Native American celebrations. Mike and the Kid climbed over the seats and went looking for sodas and chili dogs. The Gathering of Nations isn't a religious ceremony. It's a celebration of Indian solidarity and pride. The dances aren't traditional. They are contests, and some dancers make their livings at powwows. There were dances for all different age groups from the very young to the very old. The costumes are determined by style of dance rather than by nation. Some of the younger women danced in a wild and energetic style with long, beaded shawls that swung and swooped like wings. There was another dance of women of all ages who wore dresses with long fringe hanging from the sleeves. This dance was slow, rhythmic, dignified. A little girl danced with a stately, white-haired woman. The child tried to keep to the old woman's steady pace, but every now and then she broke free and leaped ahead. I examined the child through my binoculars and saw Hanna Franklin having the time of her life.

The floor cleared between dances, but motion continued in the stands as people got up to visit and look for old friends. The Kid and Mike still hadn't returned from the chili dog vendor search. The fringed women were followed by old men bent over walking sticks dancing a very slow dance. I spotted Ramona standing near the top of the stairs holding Hanna's hand. Hanna's hair was black and shining. Her eyes were enormous. Ramona wore faded jeans and a work shirt. I waved. She saw me and headed, smiling, toward our group. She stopped when she saw Nancy beside the aisle.

Nancy stood up, smoothed her hair, cleared her throat. "Hanna has grown so much," she said.

"Isn't she something?" Ramona replied.

Hanna hadn't forgotten my visit to the trailer yet and gave me a wary look.

"She's beautiful," Nancy said. "I loved your dance, Hanna."

"Thank you," Hanna said, hiding behind her mother's legs.

"It's so good to see you, Ramona," Nancy said.

"It's good to see you, Mrs. Barker," Ramona replied. She looked down to hide the emotions that blew like clouds across her face.

"We're very glad you got your job back," Eric said.

"Me, too."

"I'm sorry," Nancy said. "I'm sorry about everything."

"I . . . I miss her very much," Ramona said.

"I know." The two women hugged and cried. Eric carefully studied the old men who were finishing up their dance.

"There's Mike!" Hanna pointed up the stairs where Mike and the Kid were talking to a long-legged Anglo woman in blue jeans and a leather vest.

"Hey, Hanna," Mike yelled, but he continued talking to the woman.

The Kid climbed down to rejoin us carrying a box of chili dogs and Cokes. "Who's that Mike's talking to?" I asked him.

"A woman he knows from skiing," he said. The Kid passed around the chili dogs and Hanna took two, one in each hand. The drums started again. The beat picked up and fancy dancers came onto the floor, young men in brilliant feathers with great legs and long black hair that rippled down their backs. They whooped and leaped, dancing for the victories, dancing for the losses, dancing for the living, dancing for the dead.

"Hey, Neil. I'm glad you came." Ramona extended her hand and it felt cool and smooth and liquid in mine.